This is what happens

"An incisive reflection on how social forces constrain women's lives. ... Great for fans of Sylvia Plath, Doris Lessing's *The Golden Notebook*." *Booklife*

"I find the writing style very appealing ... An interesting mix of a memoir and a philosophical work, together with some amazing poetry. ... This is what happens ranks in my top five of books ever read." Mesca Elin, *Psychochromatic Redemption*

Thus Saith Eve

"Short, but definitely entertaining ... and serious between the lines." Lee Harmon, A Dubious Disciple Book Review

" ... a truly wonderful source of feminist fiction. In addition to being an extremely enjoyable and thought-provoking read, the monologues can also be used for audition and performance pieces." Katie M. Deaver, feminismandreligion.com

Snow White Gets Her Say

"Why isn't anyone doing this on stage? ... What a great night of theater that would be!" szferris, Librarything

"I loved the sassy voices in these stories, and the humor, even when making hard points." PJ O'Brien, Smashwords

Deare Sister

"You are clearly a writer of considerable talent, and your special ability to give expression to so many different characters, each in a uniquely appropriate style, makes your work fascinating and attractive. ... The pieces are often funny, sometimes sensitive, always creative. But they contain an enormous load of anger, and that is where I have problems. ... I know at least one feminist who would read your manuscript with delight (unfortunately she is not a publisher), who would roar with laughter in her sharing of your anger. ..." rejection letter from Black Moss Press

Particivision and other stories

"... your writing is very accomplished. ... *Particivision and other stories* is authentic, well-written, and certainly publishable. ..." rejection letter from Turnstone Press

"... engaging and clever ..." rejection letter from Lester & Orpen Dennys, Publishers

"As the title indicates, this collection of stories is about getting into the thick of things, taking sides, taking action, and speaking out loud and clear, however unpopular your opinion may be. ... refreshingly out of the ordinary." Joan McGrath, *Canadian Book Review Annual*

dreaming of kaleidoscopes

"... a top pick of poetry and is very much worth considering. ..." *Midwest Book Review*

Soliloquies: the lady doth indeed protest

"... not only dynamic, imaginative verse writing, but extremely intelligent and intuitive insight. ... I know many actresses who would love to get their hands on this material!" Joanne Zipay, Judith Shakespeare Company, NYC

"'Ophelia' is something of an oddity ... I found it curiously attractive." *Dinosaur*

UnMythed

"... A welcome relief from the usual male emphasis in this area. There is anger and truth here, not to mention courage." Eric Folsom, *Next Exit*

"... With considerable skill and much care, chris wind has extrapolated truths from mythical scenarios and reordered them in modern terms. ... Wind handles these myths with and intellect. Her voice suggests that the relationship between the consciousness of the myth-makers and modern consciousness is closer than we would think." Linda Manning, *Quarry*

"Personally, I would not publish this stuff. This is not to say it isn't publishable—it's almost flawless stylistically, perfect form and content, etc., etc. It's perverse: satirical, biting, caustic, funny. Also cruel, beyond bitter, single-minded with a terminally limited point of view, and this individual may have read Edith Hamilton's *Mythology* but she/he certainly doesn't perceive the essential meanings of these myths. Or maybe does and deliberately twists the meaning to suit the poem. Likewise, in the etymological sense. Editorial revisions suggested? None, it's perfect. Market potential/readership targets: Everyone—this is actually marketable—you could sell fill Harbourfront reading this probably. General comments: You could actually make money on this stuff." anonymous reader report for a press that rejected the ms

Satellites Out of Orbit

"*Satellites Out of Orbit* is an excellent and much recommended pick for unique fiction collections." Michael Dunford, *Midwest Book Review*

"… I also love the idea of telling the story from the woman's perspective, especially when the woman is only mentioned in passing in the official story, or not mentioned at all. …" Shana, Tales of Minor Interest

"Our editorial board loved it. Our readers said it was the most feminist thing they've read in a long time." rejection letter from publisher

As I the Shards Examine / Not Such Stuff

"*Not Such Stuff* challenges us to rethink some of our responses to Shakespeare's plays and opens up new ways of experiencing them. … " Jeff, secondat.blogspot.com

"This world premiere collection of monologs derive from eight female Shakespearian characters speaking from their hearts, describing aspects of their lives with a modern feminist sensibility. Deconstructing the traditional interpretations of some of the most fiercely fascinating female characters of all time, the playwright is able to "have at it" and the characters finally have their say. And oh, what tales they have to weave. …" Debbie Jackson, dctheatrescene.com

Let Me Entertain You

"I found this to be very powerful and visually theatrical." Ines Buchli

"I will never forget 'Let Me Entertain You.' It was brilliant." Kate Hurman

ProVocative

"Timely, thought-provoking, dark, and funny!" Kevin Holm-Hudson, WEFT

"… a great job making a point while being entertaining and interesting. … Overall this is a fine work, and worth listening to." Kevin Slick, *gajoob*

The Art of Juxtaposition

"A cross between poetry, performance art, and gripping, theatrical sound collages. … One of the most powerful pieces on the tape is 'Let Me Entertain You.' I sat stunned while listening to this composition." Myke Dyer, *Nerve*

"We found [this to be] unique, brilliant, and definitely not 'Canadian'. … We were more than impressed with the material. *The Art of Juxtaposition* is filling one of the emptier spaces in the music world with creative and intelligent music-art." rejection letter from a record company

"Controversial feminist content. You will not be unmoved." Bret Hart, *Option*

"I've just had a disturbing experience: I listened to *The Art of Juxtaposition*. Now wait a minute; Canadian musicians are not supposed to be politically aware or delve into questions regarding sexual relationships, religion, and/or sex, racism, rape. They are supposed to write nice songs that people can tap their feet to and mindlessly inebriate themselves to. You expect me to play this on my show?" Travis B., CITR

"Wind mixes biting commentary, poignant insight and dark humor while unflinchingly tackling themes such as rape, marriage (as slavery), christianity, censorship, homosexuality, the state of native Americans, and other themes, leaving no doubt about her own strong convictions upon each of these subjects. Her technique is often one in which two or more sides to each theme are juxtaposed against one another (hence, the tape's title). This is much like her *Christmas Album* with a voice just as direct and pointed. Highly recommended." Bryan Baker *gajoob*

"Thanks for *The Art of Juxtaposition* ... it really is quite a gem! Last Xmas season, after we aired 'Ave Maria' a listener stopped driving his car and phoned us from a pay phone to inquire and express delight." John Aho, CJAM

"Liked *The Art of Juxtaposition* a lot, especially the feminist critiques of the bible. I had calls from listeners both times I played 'Ave Maria.'" Bill Hsu, WEFT

"Every time I play *The Art of Juxtaposition* (several times by this point), someone calls to ask about it/you." Mars Bell, WCSB

"The work is stimulating, well-constructed, and politically apt with regard to sexual politics. (I was particularly impressed by 'I am Eve.')" Andreas Brecht Ua'Siaghail, CKCU

"We have found *The Art of Juxtaposition* to be quite imaginative and effective. When I first played it, I did not have time to listen to it before I had to be on air. When I aired it, I was transfixed by the power of it. When I had to go on mike afterward, I found I could hardly speak! To say the least, I found your work quite a refreshing change from all the fluff of commercial musicians who whine about lost love etc. Your work is intuitive, sensitive, and significant!" Erika Schengili, CFRC

"Interesting stuff here! Actually this has very little music, but it has sound bits and spoken work. Self-declared 'collage pieces of social commentary'. ...very thought-provoking and inspiring." *No Sanctuary*

more at
chriswind.net
and
chriswind.com

PARTICIVISION AND OTHER STORIES

CHRIS WIND

Magenta

Particivision and other stories
2nd Edition
© 1990, 2021 by chris wind

www.chriswind.net
www.chriswind.com

ISBN 978-1-926891-17-0 paperback
ISBN 978-1-926891-11-8 epub
ISBN 978-1-926891-58-3 pdf

Published by Magenta

This is a work of fiction. Names, characters, places, brands, media, and incidents are either the product of the author's imagination or are used fictitiously. The author acknowledges the trademarked status and trademark owners of various products referenced in this work of fiction, which have been used without permission. The publication/use of these trademarks is not authorized, associated with, or sponsored by the trademark owners.

Cover design by chris wind
Formatting and interior book design by Elizabeth Beeton

Library and Archives Canada Cataloguing in Publication

Title: Particivision and other stories / Chris Wind.
Names: wind, chris, author.
Description: Second edition. | Previously published: Sundridge, Ontario: Magenta, 1990.
Identifiers: Canadiana (print) 20210091762 | Canadiana (ebook) 20210091789 |
    ISBN 9781926891170 (softcover) | ISBN 9781926891118 (EPUB) |
    ISBN 9781926891583 (PDF)
Classification: LCC PS8595.I592 P37 2021 | DDC C813/.54—dc23

Acknowledgements

"The Great Jump-Off" *American Atheist* (Aug93), *Humanist in Canada* (Autumn 91), *Existere* (October 91)

"The School Board" *ACT* (Apr92)

"War Heroes" Northern Writers Series, CBC Radio One (Dec00)

"This Year's Hunt" Northern Writers Series, CBC Radio One (Apr00)

Thanks to the *Journal of Wild Culture, Descant, Quarry Magazine, Netherlandic Press*, and the Ontario Arts Council for their support.

Preface to second edition

Although first published in 1990, most of the stories in this collection were written during the 1980s (before computers revolutionized so many people's daily lives via internet access, laptops, smartphones, etc.). Hence, some of the stories will seem quite dated.

And although the writing is clear and concise, I see, from forty years later, that it's not particularly artful. (And some bits reveal an embarrassing naïveté.) Even so, I decided to reprint the collection (as an ebook and with the wide distribution available through print-on-demand publishing companies) because many of the points I make about how to create a better world—indeed, how to save our world—are still valid. Which is, forty years later, so very sad.

According to Ludwig von Mises, certain conditions are necessary for action to take place:

(1) people must feel uneasy with the present state of affairs
(2) they must be able to imagine a more satisfactory state of affairs
(3) they must believe that their actions can eliminate or at least reduce their uneasiness.

For people to believe that their actions can make a difference, they must first believe

(i) in a cause and effect world,
(ii) in the mind's ability to understand cause and effect relationships, and
(iii) in their ability to intervene.

Rodney F. Hiser, "How to Raise an Entrepreneur"
(Humanist in Canada Spring 1990)

✦ ✦ ✦

Action is preceded by thinking.

It is always the individual who thinks. Society does not think any more than it eats or drinks.

Thinking is linked up with language and vice versa. Concepts are embodied in terms. Language is a tool of thinking as it is a tool of social action.

Ludwig von Mises, Human Action
(Chicago: Chicago Contemporary Books, Inc., 1966)

Contents

Particivision

John Marchiano was an ordinary man. He was also an average man. He was Willy Loman now comfortable and comfortably in the middle class. It was a bit after five when he came in through the side door, took off his shoes, and hung up his coat. As he passed the den, his teen-aged son Jeff mumbled a 'Hi Dad' to the tv he was velcroed to.

"Hey Jeff, how's my favourite vegetable today?" There was no response.

"Hi dear, I'm in the kitchen," his wife, Mary, called out.

"Good," John called ahead, continuing on his way.

"What?" She poked her head out to see him. "Does that mean this is where I'm supposed to be?" she challenged.

"No," he smiled as he gave her an end-of-the-office-day hug, "it means I'm hungry. Whatcha got cookin'? Good lookin'," he added as he lifted a pot lid. He was going to say something else then, but she spoke first.

"How was your day?" she asked, sitting down at the kitchen table in the chair nearest to the stove.

"Oh, the same," he answered, moving to the liquor cupboard to prepare their drinks. Gin and tonic for her—he coloured the gin with green food colouring—she liked that—What was it he was going to say?—and a rye and soda for himself.

"Actually," he began, "I did hear something interesting today." This was it. "We have to do something about Jeff and that tv. Louise's 'beau' dropped by this morning—"

"I didn't know Louise had a 'beau'—"

"Oh yeah—some new guy from the computer store across the street, I think he's in sales—clever, a bit of a dandy—actually I have the feeling he's an unemployed actor. Anyway, I heard him telling Louise that the average Canadian watches 4.2 hours of television a day. Can you believe that? After eight hours sleep and eight hours work and a couple hours to drive and eat, there are only six hours left. *And,*" he went on with some excitement as he handed Mary her drink and sat down to join her at the table, "Jeff's age group is the worst. Fourteen- to seventeen-year-old boys watch 5.3 hours a day!"

"I knew that—I've been trying to get Jeff interested in other things for years, you know that!"

"But five hours!"

"Well, I guess at fourteen you're too old to play cops and robbers, and until eighteen you're not old enough to go out to the night spots. I expect fifteen is the very worst—not old enough to drive yet either."

"It is! How old's Jeff?" he asked without missing a beat.

"Shame on you John!" Mary reprimanded him. "Your only son—your only child—is fifteen!" He didn't remember her birthday either. "Is it the same for girls, did he say? What's his name?"

"No—I mean no he didn't say. I don't know. Jerry." He took a swallow from his drink. "If only Jeff were interested in sports … He joined the computer club didn't he? After we bought him the Atari last Christmas? And all those games!"

"Yes, he joined. But he quit a month later. I'm sure I told you."

"But why? He loves that computer! He spends almost as much time with the tv hooked into one of those games as he does with the tv alone, doesn't he?"

"Yes—that's just it. He only likes the games. In the computer club, they get into programming and stuff like that. He says he's not interested."

"Well he'd better *get* interested! See, Jerry left a report with Louise—probably to impress her—but she gave it to me, thinking that because we have Jeff I'd be interested. Besides," he added, "I don't think she can read."

"John!"

"Well she sure as hell can't add! If I trusted her work, the company would be offering auto policies for a premium of $56 per year! Anyway, I read the report on my lunch."

"And?"

"Well it was a really interesting report. Full of lots of conjecture, I know," he waved his hand as if to dismiss parts of it, "but it had a profile on the ten most popular shows and described in detail the television-watching process."

"What process? You just sit there."

"Exactly. So it encourages passivity. And in every single show, there was conflict followed by favourable resolution. So the kid learns that good wins out over bad without him having to do anything. Without his help, without his interference, his involvement—everyone will live happily ever after! Problems solve themselves!"

Mary had gotten up to stir the stew. "It's a dangerous lesson, isn't it?" she said.

"Yes! What are we going to do about it?"

"Well, as always, I think setting an example—"

"We'll have a family discussion," he cut her off, "we'll talk with him, make him see what's happening."

Mary didn't say anything.

"Jeff?" John called toward the den. no response. "Jeff—" he tried again, louder.

"What?" A whine, defensive.

"Could you please come out here? Your mother and I would like to talk with you."

"Now?" irritated.

"Yes, now!"

"But I'm in the middle of 'Family Ties'! Can't it wait till it's over?"

As soon as John finished his stew, he half-tossed his knife and fork onto his plate and shoved it away, toward the center of the table. It was a habit, a mannerism—a manner—that bothered Mary. But in seventeen years, she hadn't quite figured out why. Sometimes she thought it was the 'Finished!' feeling of it, as if eating a meal she had prepared was a race—or a chore. And that bothered her. But more often, she thought she recognized in the gesture an 'I don't want anything (more) to do with things that don't concern me' attitude. It was less that he was *finished* with the meal than that *he* was finished with it. And that bothered her even more.

"What we wanted to talk to you about," John began, "was how much you watch tv." No response. "Do you know how many hours a day you spend watching that thing?"

"5.3."

John raised his eyebrows at Mary.

"We took it in school. 'The average Canadian watches 4.2 hours of television per day. Fourteen- to seventeen-year-olds watch 5.3 hours of television per day.'"

"Well then," this was encouraging, Jeff was aware of the problem.

"What did they teach you about the effect it has on you?"

"It can make you insensitive to violence."

"Well yes, there's that." John hadn't thought of that. Was that in the report? "Anything else?" he asked.

"It's mostly white people and a lot of them are rich."

That too. But this was the wrong direction. He tried again.

"Do you ever raise your hand in class, Jeff?"

"What do you mean?"

"Well, I mean do you participate in class, do you discuss things with the teacher or with the other students—do you get involved?"

"Sometimes. Most of the time, they just say stuff and we write it down. Or we have to copy it from the board. No," he amended, "actually only Ms. Jones does that. Mostly we get hand-outs."

"Hand-outs?" Charity?

"Yeah, like they prepare the notes for us and then just photocopy them and hand them out. We're supposed to put them in our notebooks. But sometimes they don't even punch the holes. We have to do that ourselves. It's a real pain. There's never a hole-puncher around."

This wasn't going well. "What about projects?"

"What about them?"

"Do you ever do projects? I mean, get up, move around, make something—"

"Make something? Like in shop? Yeah. And art. But I'm dropping that next year."

"No, I mean like—well—I remember back in school I did a project on road construction. My partner and I built a road—a model, I mean. We made a box with glass in the one side so you could see the cross-section—there were layers of gravel and dirt and cement somewhere, I think—"

"That's grade school stuff, dad. In high school you do essays."

"I think what your father's trying to get at, Jeff, is the doing. He's—we're afraid that watching so much television is turning you—getting you into the habit of *not* doing. Not doing anything. Being passive—"

"What did you want me to do?" Jeff asked, puzzled.

"Well—anything! Problems don't solve themselves, Jeff, you have to do something about them." John picked up the ball again.

Jeff was silent. "Is there a problem?"

It wasn't going well again. "Well, there's lots! Don't you read the paper? Do they have you read the paper in school?"

"Oh you mean like the nuclear thing and the environment—"

"Well—yes, okay, things like that!"

Jeff was quiet. "So you're blaming that on me too."

John was stunned. "What?"

Jeff was suddenly upset. "We get that all day at school! Mercury poisoning the fish, lead in the air, the ozone layer and the stuff in our fridge and our air conditioner and styrofoam before McDonalds stopped using it, and the greenhouse effect because of the carbon dioxide because of all the cars, and the tritium being sold by Canada to other countries— Well it's not my fault, why should I have to do anything about it and what can I do anyway? *I* don't have the big bucks, *I'm* not in power—I don't— I can't even drive a car yet! And I don't see *you* doing anything about it!" he glared at his dad.

"Well," John grasped at straws, "I'm busy earning a living, supporting you two." There was silence. "Your mother does things," he pacified. "She's always off to one meeting or another, petitions, and …" He trailed off.

"Yeah. And a big difference it's making too." Jeff got up and left the table.

This hadn't gone well at all.

A few weeks later when John came home, he had a package for Jeff. A solution to the problem. He took off his shoes, hung up his coat, and waltzed into the den.

"Here," he set the package on the small table beside Jeff, who was sitting on the couch watching tv. "It's the very latest thing apparently. Mary?" he called out, "Have you got a minute?"

"Coming!" she answered from upstairs. The sound of her footsteps followed.

"Jerry brought it over today to show Louise," he explained to her, as soon as she had come into the den, "and I bought it on the spot." He looked back at Jeff, "It's sort of a marriage between computers and television—you oughta love it." He grinned like a father who knows best.

Jeff had unwrapped the package and was holding a piece of computer software.

"See," John pointed to the specifications written on the box, "it's compatible with Atari, McIntosh, IBM, and Commodore. And Hitachi, Zenith, Electrohome, and RCA. Give it a try!"

While Jeff connected the computer to the television, Mary took the box from John and read aloud the name of the program: "'Particivision'." Then she read the words written underneath like a famous quote: "'Believing in your own impotence is the first step toward death.'"

"What does that mean?" Jeff asked from behind the tv.

"It—"

"I don't know," John interrupted, impatient with excitement, "just put the thing in and we'll see."

Jeff inserted the Particivision cartridge. Nothing happened.

"All the wires plugged in tightly?" Mary asked. Jeff checked. They were.

"Eject it and try it again," John suggested, annoyed. Jeff did so. Still nothing.

"Well, supper's ready. Let's eat and have a look at it later."

"Yeah, okay, I'll read the manual after supper." If nothing else, Jeff wanted to get it to work, to see what it did.

"Damn that Jerry, if he sold me a bum piece—"

"Calm down, John. Let Jeff read the manual. He'll figure it out."

She winked at her son. Jeff smiled a thanks, and they headed out to the kitchen.

John mixed their drinks to have during the meal, while Mary took a meat loaf out of the oven and put the potatoes and corn into serving bowls. Dinner chat was usual, inconsequential. Jeff ate his food then excused himself.

Half an hour later, just as the dishes were being put away, he called out triumphantly. "I got it!"

John and Mary went into the den. The television was on; John recognized the regular 6:30 show, 'Cheers'. He looked at Jeff for an explanation.

"We had it hooked up wrong."

"But you know how—"

"No, this one is connected differently. There was an extra wire in the box that goes from here to here," he pointed. "It has a sort of mini-descrambling thing in the middle. At least I think that's what it does. Sort of." Then he held up a sheet of paper. "Because you bought the program, we're automatically subscribers to this newsletter too. This is the first issue. We send in our address, and they'll send us all the back issues to get us up to date. But this is from January, so we're only a couple months behind."

"Let me see that," John reached for the newsletter.

"It actually looks really neat. It's a sort of interference program. With certain television shows, there are certain moves or choices available. And people who are hooked up with the program, play—or send—their moves with their joysticks."

"Then what happens?" Mary asked.

"Well it says that the show is then directed by the viewers' moves. I'm not sure how that happens."

"Sounds kind of like the parlour walls in *Fahrenheit 451*," Mary commented. But seeing Jeff's blank face, she realized he hadn't taken the novel yet.

"You'd think it'd be pretty expensive for a show to have two endings in the can and then broadcast the one the people at home pick," John couldn't believe it.

"Yeah ..." Jeff agreed.

"We can do this with all the shows?" Mary asked, incredulous.

"No, that's a bit of the catch," he reached out to his father and turned the newsletter over in his hands, then pointed to a list. "Only 'The Edison Twins' has 'Particivision'." He shrugged his shoulders, anticipating his dad's anger.

"Just one show? I paid good money for this! And it only works for one show?" John was outraged. "Damn that Jerry! 'State-of-the-art pioneering program' my foot!" He turned to Jeff. "And what's 'The Edison Twins'? Is that a show you watch?" he demanded.

"Well, no," Jeff mumbled. "It's a bit hokey. It's on Saturday afternoons." John threw the newsletter onto the couch and left the room.

"Remember when stereo tv first came out?" Jeff called after him hopefully. "'Miami Vice' was the only show to have it, but others joined ..."

"But now that's become just a passing fad, right?" Mary asked.

"Well, yeah," Jeff admitted. "Can I send in our address anyway?"

"Oh sure," Mary encouraged, "might as well. Your father's paid for it."

That Saturday, Jeff wasn't doing anything much, so he figured he may as well watch 'The Edison Twins'. As he had said, it was pretty hokey. At the last moment in a science fair, Tom Edison's project fell apart because a transformer failed. The electronics store had closed early, but it was easy enough to get in through the window. So he asked his sister to go to the store, climb in, and get a replacement transformer. He gave her a note to leave and the money to pay for it. But it was still 'break and enter' and she didn't really want to do it. And yet, she knew Tom's project had a good chance of winning; without the transformer he wouldn't even place.

There was nothing unusual about the show, and Jeff thought maybe the Particivision program didn't work after all. But then just before the last commercial break, a voice sort of like a cross between R2D2 and Hal came on and said "Move your joystick to the upward position to send her to the store, to the downward position to have her refuse, to the left to have him explain to the judges and request and be granted an extension, and to the right for him to explain and be denied an extension." The message was repeated twice, and then a commercial about toothpaste came on.

Jeff moved his joystick to the left. After two more commercials, for O'Henry and Tonka toys, the show returned. Tom's sister refused. He explained his problem to the judges and they granted an extension. Jeff cheered.

When his mother came in to see what he was yelling about, he explained what had happened, how Particivision worked.

"Good for you!" She was impressed—with the program *and* with her son's choice. "I think I would have chosen to do the same."

"I guess there must've been a tie between options two and three."

"I wonder what would've happened if the tie had been between options one and three. I guess she would have gone to the store and in the meantime he would have explained to the judges—"

"Yeah but what if there was a tie between options one and two— what then?"

"I don't know," she said. "Why don't you write and ask?"

The suggestion delighted him. "Yeah! Okay, I will!"

"Still," she added, "how can they do that? They must have half a dozen endings pre-filmed. The money!"

"Maybe it's worth it in increased viewing."

"It must be."

Jeff was excited, he felt good. Mary noticed that, smiled, and left the room.

About a week and a half later, Jeff received a large manilla envelope in the mail. The Particivision newsletters. The newsletter was weekly, not monthly as he had thought, so there were about fourteen to go through. And it had grown in length. He saw that the later issues were several pages long. He took the pile into the den and started reading.

On the back page of the second issue, there was sort of a statistics report. 'The Edison Twins' was listed with a broadcast date of January 13. That must've been the first one. Beside it was the total number of people that had Particivision—112 at that time. And then the breakdown of the moves: 33 (74%) had chosen option one, 27 (24%) had chosen option two, and 2 (2%) had not participated. Only two options when it first started, he noticed.

He turned over the single piece of paper. On the front was a list of 'New Shows' and beside it, 'Participating Shows to Date'. In the week of January 13, the show 'Airwaves' had been added.

Jeff pulled out the most recent issue, dated April 21. Participating shows to date were 'The Edison Twins', 'Airwaves', 'The Polka Dot Door', 'Danger Bay', a couple he didn't recognize, and 'Knight Rider'. 'Knight Rider'? He thought that show had been cancelled long ago. It was the one with that computer-intelligent car—Kitt? Maybe this was a way to try to revive the show. He wondered if reruns could be made into Particivision shows or if they had to produce from scratch. There was another column of 'Shows under Consideration'. 'Hooperman' was a maybe. He did watch that. Actually he had watched 'Knight Rider' a lot when it was on too. And though he wasn't a great fan of 'Airwaves' or 'Danger Bay', they weren't quite as bad as 'The Edison Twins'.

He turned to the back page of the issue. Woh—membership was up from 112 to 7,260! Jeff wondered how quickly computer games had caught on. He also saw though that average participation rate had decreased—it was down from 98% to 80%. Still, he thought, that's a lot. considering. And he was right about the show he'd participated in. 31% had chosen option two, her refusal, and 31% had chosen that he explain and get an extension. Only 10% had chosen to explain and get no extension, and 28% had chosen for her to break in to the store. That surprised him.

On the second page, Jeff found a 'Letters' section. He read it with interest. Most people wrote in to say what a great idea Particivision was, and many suggested shows that should join: 'Dallas', 'The Young and Restless', 'The Cosby Show', 'Romper Room', 'Tour of Duty'— That would be interesting. He wondered if people would choose not to fire, not to obey the commands …

He worked his way through the rest of the issues in chronological order. He saw that the increase in membership was pretty steady, and that the number of choices went from two to three to four. He saw that 'The Polka Dot Door' had the highest participation rate—97%. He thought about that. It was a kids' show. 'Knight Rider' was second, with 88%. He saw that in some cases the moves were evenly spread among the options, and in other cases there was a clear majority. In one case, one option got no votes at all. That was a 'Danger Bay' episode in February. He wondered what the option was. He decided to write a letter to the newsletter to see if he could find out.

He also discovered—and it shouldn't have surprised him—that the newsletter was available as an on-line bulletin board. That meant he could find out the scores, the breakdown, almost as the choices were made. And he could know right away which shows had joined. But he needed a modem. They were a bit more expensive than what his dad had paid for the program. Quite a bit actually. But they could be used for other things too. Well, he decided, it wouldn't hurt to ask.

As the weeks passed, Jeff started watching television more ... more actively. He put red boxes around all of the Particivision shows when the tv guide came. He missed only 'The Polka Dot Door' and sometimes 'The Edison Twins'. Actually, he grew to like that show. 'Airwaves' and 'Danger Bay' were okay too. Some episodes had boring and trivial choices, but some required really important decisions. He found it hard sometimes to make up his mind quickly at the end. So he started anticipating the choice and evaluating things that happened throughout the show, so he had an opinion ready by the time he had to choose.

Part way through the summer, one show had two things to decide about. That kind of threw him, because the first decision didn't turn out as he had chosen, so he had to make a decision at the end about a situation he didn't agree with to begin with. That was kind of hard.

And later on, one decision in particular really interested and really bothered him. Jonah, in 'Danger Bay', had to decide whether or not to be part of a tv commercial being shot at his school: the company would pay an extravagant amount of money to each of five students—Jonah was chosen to be one of them—and if the student gave his payment to a special oil spill clean-up fund, the company would match the amount with a contribution of its own. But the commercial was really stupid: he and the other four guys had to lounge like sexy dudes on the school steps and watch a sexy girl walk by; the ad was for vitamins and the 'punch line' was 'Vitamins make you grow—up'. He chose to have Jonah do the commercial, but the story ended with his deciding not to do it.

After that one, Jeff checked the mail every day for the newsletter (his father had said no to the modem). When it finally came, he immediately turned to the back page.

"Shit!" he shouted angrily and threw it onto the kitchen table.

"Jeff!" Mary turned from the stove. Her reprimand was for his language. But it might have also been for the way he had become so involved with Particivision. She wasn't sure.

"Just three more people had to agree with me, and Jonah would've done the commercial. And over 2,000 people abstained!" he cried out, "Too lazy to participate!"

"Maybe some of them really couldn't make up their minds."

"No—well maybe, but the participation rate has been slowly decreasing." He pointed to the overall average on the back page. "Look. It's dropped to 72%. People just don't care!"

"About what?" John asked, entering the kitchen. He had just come home.

"Anything!" Jeff said with exasperation, as he brushed past him heading toward the den.

John raised his eyebrows at Mary for an explanation. She told him about the 'Danger Bay' episode.

"He's hooked on the stuff, Mary—addicted," he said, mixing their drinks.

"So?" Mary asked, eager to explore this and find out where she stood. "He was also addicted to computer games."

"Yes," John agreed, "but he was never this ... this fanatic about the computer games!"

"That's true," she had to admit. "But then, the decisions were never this important. He's acting on his values now, his beliefs, his opinions. There's a moral dimension to his participation now."

"But he's changed, Mary. He's more ... more volatile!"

"I know ... But he's using his mind now, he's thinking, and feeling. And—" she hesitated, though the more she spoke, the more certain she was of her approval.

"And?"

"And I think he's learning the power of numbers. He's learning what a difference a single voice *can* make."

"I don't know … It makes me uneasy."

"You'd rather he go back to being your 'favourite vegetable'?"

"Well," he gave her drink one last stir before handing it to her, "no, I guess not."

In the den, still smouldering, Jeff flipped through the rest of the newsletter. Membership was up a bit, there were no new shows; he read the breakdowns for the other shows, and he read the letters. Then he noticed an article that was called 'It's only make-believe.' He read it through, twice. Basically it argued that the participation rate was decreasing because the situations, choices, and outcomes were only make-believe. The stuff wasn't real, so people didn't really care. Jeff thought there might be something to this. But he also knew that more people watched tv than voted or gave blood. He knew his dad, for instance, would rather stay home and watch 'Night Heat' than go with his mom to an Eco-Action meeting. And yet, he knew that if the situations on Particivision *were* real, *he'd* be a lot more involved. Though, he realized then, he was pretty involved now. The article ended with a suggestion to the makers of Particivision: make one of the episodes real and see what happens. Wow. That *would* be interesting. But they probably wouldn't do it. How could they?

Another school year had started, Jeff was now in grade eleven, and things continued pretty much as they had been. John continued to go to work every day and read the newspaper in front of the tv at night. Occasionally, when 'Danger Bay' or 'Knight Rider' was on, Jeff talked his dad into making the choice instead of him. John would mumble the option of his choice from behind his newspaper so Jeff could move the joystick, but Jeff insisted he do it himself. He felt silly, but as Mary had said, they should set a good example, so he humoured the boy. On the few occasions that this happened, Jeff noted that his dad never even bothered to pay much attention to the outcome.

Mary continued to manage the household and be active in three or four groups: she went to meetings, organized fund-raisers, circulated petitions. More often than John, she would 'watch' or 'play' or 'do' particivision with Jeff. She especially enjoyed 'The Edible Woman', a new series based on some novel by Margaret Atwood.

Then something happened. Jeff was watching an episode of 'Knight Rider', and the choice involved a spiked two-by-four laid across the road by the enemy: should Michael try to stop in time, should he swerve and go over the cliff, or should he drive over the board. Jeff decided that he couldn't stop in time; they were travelling at over 300 km/h. Going over the cliff would probably mean death, unless Kitt had wings. So he decided to go over the board; he figured the spikes wouldn't pierce Kitt's tires because they were probably made of some 'supertech' material. He went into the kitchen to get another bowl of chips.

When he came back, Michael was in the hospital, paralyzed from the waist down.

"What?" Jeff couldn't believe it. He turned the volume up, as if that would change what had happened.

Michael had driven over the board; the spikes *had* pierced the tires. He lost control of the car, and it went over the cliff. The car was totalled, but of course it could be rebuilt. "But it won't be the same," Michael was crying. "He'll never be the same Kitt again!" He was actually crying.

"Neither will you," the doctor said evenly. "I'm afraid the accident severed your spine at a crucial vertebra. The paralysis is permanent."

Jeff couldn't believe it. This didn't happen, not to the Knight Rider.

"Jeff!" he heard his mother call. "Supper!" He turned the tv off and went in to the kitchen to eat.

As he told his parents what had happened, he became more and more agitated.

"It's my fault! I voted to go over the board!"

"So did a lot of other people, dear." Mary was concerned. Jeff was unusually upset. Surely he knew Michael was only a tv character. But then she recalled that Jeff had been devoted to this show when it originally came out; he would've been only ten or eleven at the time.

"But if I'd tried to stop instead, maybe—"

"There's a ward full of maybes and ifs in every hospital, Jeff," Mary said. "It *does* happen. That's one of the risks of fast driving."

"What, are you turning this into a lesson on dangerous driving?" He acted as if she was making light of it all.

"Well—"

"Is that all it is to you?"

"Just you wait till next week," John was saying. "There'll be a choice about whether or not the doctor was wrong. Unless they want an 'Ironsides' replacement or a 'Longstreet'. Come to think of it, both are off the air. Maybe they figure the market's right for another disabled hero."

"What are you talking about?" Jeff asked, sullen at being led off track.

"'Ironsides' is an old tv show, it had Raymond Burr in it—'Perry Mason'?"

Jeff shook his head.

"Well the main character was confined to a wheelchair. And in 'Longstreet' the hero was blind."

"Oh," Jeff said, seeming to relax a little, "cops and robbers shows too?"

"More or less," Mary answered.

But in the following week's episode, there was no choice about whether or not the doctor was mistaken. In fact, there was no choice at all in the whole program. Not even about the colour of Michael's wheelchair.

The show had changed. Kitt wasn't rebuilt yet, and Michael wasn't getting into any adventures. Unless you could call going to a grocery store with no ramps, a turnstile entrance, and 22" wide checkouts an adventure. And his personality had changed. Michael wasn't— He wasn't cool anymore, Jeff realized. He watched the show for a few more episodes. Kitt's cousin arrived, C.V. (short for W.C.C.I.V., a Wheelchair Compatible Computer Interfaced Van), then he stopped watching it. It wasn't long before he stopped participating in the other shows as well.

Mary asked him about it one day. He shrugged it off.

"Look Jeff, you made a decision. You were wrong. Or at least the consequences were painful. That happens."

"I know."

"Usually without such drastic consequences."

"I know."

"And often the consequences are personal. At least in this case, it didn't really affect you. Jeff, it's make-believe, don't forget that."

"I know."

A month later, 'MacGyver' became part of the Particivision roster. It was Jeff's favourite show. He liked MacGyver. The guy was so resourceful. He had a physics degree or something, but was as far from the brainy nerd stereotype as Jeff could imagine. And he didn't carry a weapon. In fact, he didn't use violence at all to solve his problems. Well, he didn't use direct violence. He did 'intervene'—people did get hurt because of what he did—but it was really because of what they themselves did. MacGyver just rigged the results. And he drove a jeep. That was a plus. And there was hardly ever a 'romantic interest' subplot. Another plus, as far as Jeff was concerned. And so, eventually, Jeff began to participate again.

John was concerned. He knew how much Jeff liked MacGyver. "What if he chooses wrong again?" he asked Mary. "Remember what happened with that 'Knight Rider' thing."

"What happened? He learned what a responsibility it is, to make a decision." She had given this Particivision thing a lot of thought. "And he's learning in a safe environment. I mean, vicariously. None of this is quite real, remember."

At first Jeff got involved just with 'MacGyver'. But after a while, he picked up again with all of the other shows too. Except 'Knight Rider'. Sometimes he chose this option, sometimes that. A couple of times, he couldn't decide. A couple of times, he couldn't decide fast enough. And a couple of times, he made a mistake. Though none affected him quite as much as that first one with 'Knight Rider'.

And then something else happened. The Particivision newsletter announced that an upcoming episode would be real.

"How can they do that?" Jeff asked him mom.

"I don't know," Mary was intrigued. "I guess we'll have to wait and see. When is it?"

"October 23, 5:30, 'Danger Bay'."

Mary went to mark it on the calendar. "Oh."

"What?" Jeff got up from the kitchen table to look at the calendar.

"You have a dentist appointment at 4:30 that day—"

"Change it!" Mary turned to him sharply. He blushed. It *had* sounded like an order.

"Well, you may still be home in time. We have an hour."

"Yeah, but I also might not be. *Can't* we change it?"

"No, I don't think so. You know these appointments are made six months in advance ..."

"It's only a check-up!"

She paused. Clearly this was important to Jeff. As she thought it should be. She didn't want to discourage his interest, his willingness to be involved in *real* decision-making.

So, she picked up the phone and called Dr. Singh's office. Jeff stood close by her elbow.

"Hello, this is Mary Benson calling. My son Jeff has an appointment on October 23 at 4:30, and I'm wondering if we could change that. Yes. I see. Four months? No. Yes. All right, thanks anyway." She hung up the phone.

"He's booked solid for four months."

"Damn!" Jeff hit the door frame. "I won't go," he decided.

"Jeff—"

"No! This is more important."

Mary looked at her son. Half a year ago, he wouldn't have cared. About anything. Now he was even establishing priorities.

"What about a proxy vote? Your father will be home. Talk to him. Ask him to vote for you if you don't make it home in time. And if you do, well, there's no problem."

Jeff thought about it. "Do you think he would?"

"You don't know till you ask him."

So, at suppertime, Jeff explained the situation and asked his father if he'd choose for him—if he didn't make it home in time.

"How can they make it real?"

"We don't know ..."

"Will you do it?" Jeff asked, again, urgently.

"Sure, sure ..." John ate another mouthful of mashed potatoes.

"Great! Thanks dad!" It was settled.

"Can you imagine if the parliamentary sessions hooked into Particivision?"

Mary mused aloud.

At 6:13 p.m., Jeff burst through the front door and ran into the den. No one was there. His father wasn't there. The tv was off.

"Dad?" he called, running back through the house. He collided with his mother in the hallway.

"Where's Dad? He's not in the den!"

"I don't know, Jeff, I just got here too remember?" She had been putting up with his anxiety since 4:00 when she had picked up him at school. Nevertheless, and therefore, she too began to look for John. They found him in the back yard, raking up the leaves.

"Dad, what happened?" Jeff ran out and almost pounced on his father.

"Nothing, what's wrong?" John was puzzled.

"'Danger Bay!' What happened? What were the options?!"

"John—you—" Mary knew it before Jeff.

"Oops." John looked at Jeff who then realized his father had forgotten.

"Oops?" he exploded. "The first real choice— You said you would!" He kicked at the pile of leaves. "And all you can say is oops?"

"Jeff, I'm sorry," John said, then moved to continue raking.

"But this was real!" he grabbed at the rake. "And it might have been important!"

John was taken aback. "To you," he struggled to stay calm. "It might have been important to you."

"Why wasn't it important to *you*?" he shouted. "What *is* important to you?" He stormed toward the house and slammed the door.

"John, how *could* you—" Mary started to say, but then went after Jeff.

"Jeff?" she called, once inside the house. "Jeff?"

"Leave me alone!" he yelled from his bedroom upstairs.

Supper was tense, and silent.

Finally Jeff spoke, to his mother. "I called Sandy. There was a seal that needed expensive surgery. The aquarium could do it, but only with public approval, because they'd have to use money from the Ministry, the taxpayers would be paying for it."

"Sandy chose yes to the operation?" John tried to appease with interest.

"No. Sandy had track practice. Her mom voted," he glared at his father, "—yes."

John had had enough. "Don't you dare give me that look! Sandy's mother probably doesn't have a job all day. Like your mother, she has the time and energy to get involved, to go to all those meetings and bake sales and what have you." Mary looked up from her plate in protest, but he ignored her. "I don't have the time to be a bleeding heart!"

"Sandy's mom works," she quietly stated.

"And I'd rather have a bleeding heart than one that's made of stone!" Jeff cried out.

"Now listen here, this has gone far enough, I do care—"

"You do not! Look at you! You sell insurance! Your job depends on bad things happening! So of course you don't do anything to make sure good things happen!"

"Jeff, that's enough," Mary warned, but he continued.

"You'd probably vote against immortality because look at all the money you'd lose in life insurance policies!" He threw his knife and fork onto his dinner plate and left the table.

"It was insurance companies that brought in seat belts, young man!" John yelled after his son.

"Yeah, to save money, not lives!" Jeff screamed back.

All three were shocked to read the paper the next day. A young seal had died at the Vancouver Aquarium 'because public approval had not been obtained to use Ministry monies for the complex and expensive life-saving surgery that was required'. Nothing more was said.

Months passed. Every now and then a real Particivision would be announced and Jeff would be sure to be there. If he couldn't—once he had to take his driver's test—Mary would make the choice.

Jeff continued to read the newsletters, which by now had become a small newspaper. He noticed that the participation rate shot up every time the episode—or choice—was real. He pointed this out to his mother.

"I guess I was wrong. People do care," he said.

"Or we're more apt to do something when we're sure that what we do will have an effect."

After a while he said, "You know, I think I understand the box now."

"The box?"

"Yeah. The inscription or whatever: 'Believing in your own impotence is the first step toward death.' When you don't think you can do anything about it, your heart dies because you stop caring, you stop feeling—because otherwise it hurts too much. And your mind dies because you stop thinking—of solutions, alternatives. And your body dies from simple inactivity." Mary listened, amazed. He went on, "And if people die, then the planet will die too. With a bang if it's because of a nuclear thing, with a whimper if it's because of the environment."

Then suddenly there weren't any more real episodes.

"I wonder why," Jeff asked out loud.

"Maybe a legal problem?" Mary suggested.

"Maybe it costs too much," John said.

Nevertheless, Jeff continued to watch and make moves for 'Airwaves', 'Danger Bay', 'The Edison Twins', 'MacGyver', and 'Knight Rider'. 'Night Heat' had also joined the list, but the decisions to be made on that show were always incredibly stupid or incredibly trivial—like 'Should Jambone hustle the new detective or not?'

John was an avid fan of that one, however, and one night, much to his surprise, the episode focussed on Nikki's pregnancy: O'Brien didn't know whether or not he wanted a baby, and Nikki didn't want it if O'Brien didn't know and/or if he intended to continue being a cop. O'Brien couldn't imagine not being a cop, but he also didn't want to lose Nikki. Suddenly John was asked to decide. He didn't know either. One commercial passed. He became hot and sweaty looking at the joystick. Another commercial passed. How could he decide about O'Brien's kid, he hadn't even really decided about his own, it had just happened. And as for being a cop, well it beat the hell out of selling insurance. But if he didn't choose—he heard Jeff's voice, full of derision: he'd be an 'abstainer'. He shut the tv off in anger.

One morning at breakfast, John casually noted that a certain church in Toronto was going to be torn down to make room for a new office-retail building. Jeff paused over his cereal.

"Where is it?"

"Bloor Street."

"It's not the St. Paul Trinity United Church, is it?" He was almost afraid to ask.

"Why, yes. Why?" Jeff had quickly left the table. He returned with a stack of old Particivision newsletters.

"That was the choice on 'Airwaves' Tuesday night. I didn't know it was a real one. I don't remember it being announced." He began to look carefully, but quickly, through the newsletters for mention of it. Mary grabbed one and also began reading. John reluctantly helped. Ten minutes later they had gone through the last two months. There was no mention of it.

"Maybe it was an error, an omission," John said.

"Yeah … maybe."

But it happened again. And then again.

The three of them were in the den watching 'The Edible Woman'.

"This is so frustrating," Jeff commented, "not knowing if this is real or not."

"It's just a ploy to increase viewing," John muttered.

Suddenly Mary thought she understood. "Maybe that's the point."

"What?"

"Well, that's life. I mean we never know for sure if what we're going to do will really make a difference."

"Yeah … I can see that," Jeff said slowly, "but you may as well believe that it will. 'Perception is more important than reality.' Yeah!" He had made a connection.

"What?" John was roused from reading the paper. "Where'd you hear that?"

"In school. Some psychologist or philosopher said it. It means that what you *believe* or *perceive* to be true is ultimately more important than what really *is* true."

"Well, more important regarding motivation, maybe," Mary cautioned, "but consequences still unfold according to the *reality* of the incident, not according to what you *believed* about it."

"Yeah, I guess that's true," Jeff conceded. "At least, I guess I *believe* it to be true," he grinned at her.

"What do your stats indicate about participation now?" Mary seemed to change the subject.

"What do you mean?

"Well now that some of these are real and some aren't, but we never know— Are people opting out, or is participation increasing, or fluctuating, or what?"

"Well," he thought back, "when it was all make-believe, it went from about 98% right at the beginning when it started and it was all new and exciting to everyone—"

"And everyone had just forked out the money for it," John interjected.

"Yeah," he accepted his father's point, then resumed, "it went from 98% to around 64%. Though every time a new show was added, it went up a bit."

"Okay …"

"But over, I don't know, six to eight months maybe, it kept decreasing."

"Then when the episodes were real?"

"Then it went back up to somewhere in the 90s for the real ones."

"And for the make-believes?"

"They were down … to the 60s, I think." He paused, reconsidering. "No, you're right. I never realized that. Then the make-believes were way down, some were even in the 40s."

"And now?"

"Now I think it's been around 70%," he grabbed a few of the latest issues. "No—high 70s and 80s."

"That's what I thought," she said. "We're like those rats on behavioural modification programs."

"What?" Both John and Jeff turned to her.

"When you teach rats to do something, you can reward them every time they get it right, or at regular intervals, say every third time they get it right, or at random, sometimes they'd get a pellet for doing it right and sometimes they wouldn't, they never knew for sure. They learned best in the last situation." Mary smiled. She admired Particivision's pedagogical strategy. John just grunted. He didn't like being a rat, especially a manipulated one. And Jeff—Jeff had put his hand on the joystick, ready.

Then just when they thought they had it all figured out, something else happened. Another real episode was announced in advance.

"This is weird," Jeff said as he read it aloud. "They haven't done this for months! 'There will be a real episode on 'Night Heat', December 20, of great global importance.' Why would they start announcing again?"

"Maybe they want to make sure this one gets a 90s participation rate," Mary suggested. She wondered what it could be. A question of outlawing leaded gas? Would they, *could* they actually legislate on the basis of the Particivision scores? Of course not.

"Yeah, but 'Night Heat'?"

"Well, in spite of everything, that show probably has the highest viewing." A call to boycott maybe? Consumer products manufactured by nuclear arms contractors?

"What's that 'in spite of everything' supposed to mean?" John asked.

"But something of 'great global importance'? On 'Night Heat'?" Jeff persisted.

"Give the show a break! It's not that bad!" John came to O'Brien's defense.

"Yeah, Nikki's been having a great influence on O'Brien," Mary offered. "And that new woman, in forensics? She's showing what Jambone's made of."

"Yeah, but then they've got that other bozo, that narc cop with so many problems I can't begin—"

"Cut it out, both of you! It's the best thing since 'Mannix' and you know it!"

Mary and Jeff grinned at each other and shrugged their shoulders.

"I saw that." John grinned too in spite of himself.

"Oh no," Jeff suddenly cried when he had continued reading.

"What?"

"Not another dentist appointment," John muttered.

"No, it's the school ski trip to Quebec!"

"And *you* are—" John looked at Mary.

"—one of the chaperones, yes."

"Look Dad, if you can't, just say so, I won't go."

"You'd give up a ski trip to Mont Blanc?" John was amazed.

"Yes." Without hesitation. "Dad?"

"I'm sure another parent would be glad to substitute for—"

"I watch 'Night Heat' all the time anyway, you know that," John assured his son.

"Yeah, but will you— Will you get involved?" Jeff asked.

Did he know about that one time he'd tried to? He hadn't managed to even touch the joystick. Then or since.

"Dad, it's important." Jeff pressed for a commitment.

"John?" Mary too wanted to hear. "We need to know."

"What if I make a choice you don't agree with?" John asked.

"Well," Jeff shyly grinned, "better to have done wrong than never to have done at all."

"Actually," Mary said, "I think we're at the point where to do nothing *is* to do wrong. Besides," she added, "I think we agree more than we disagree on matters of 'great global importance'."

"All right! Yes! Yes, I'll do it!" He waved them off like a couple of mosquitoes. But as soon as he said it, he felt— He felt good.

"Promise?" Jeff insisted.

John Marchiano looked at Mary, then at Jeff. "Yes," he said. "Promise."

This Year's Hunt

They argued over who was going to go in whose truck again this year. Like last year. And the year before. Every October on this particular Friday, they'd stand in front of Smithy's house and bicker.

"No way," Bruce said to Ike, "you take Archie this year." He started unbuttoning his red plaid hunting jacket. "As soon as we pull onto the 401, he falls asleep and snores so fuckin' loud you can't even hear the radio." He walked around to open the back of his GM, threw his jacket inside, and stared at Ike.

Ike had pulled in behind Bruce and was sitting sideways in the driver's seat with the door open. He didn't seem to respond one way or the other to Bruce. Bruce could be a real asshole sometimes.

Chuck, crouched down on the other side of Bruce's truck, checking the air pressure of the tires, grinned. He and Bruce grew up together, and they knew each other better than most brothers did. "When did you start listening to the radio again, Brucey?" he called over.

"Chuck you shut up," Bruce warned.

"What's this? You don't listen to the radio anymore?" Tim took the bait. He was leaning against the front of Ike's truck, dressed in a sweatshirt, jeans, and running shoes. He was a numbers cruncher, and could've been fat and out of shape, but he got hooked on running five years ago. He was a lean man now, almost stringy. He'd run three marathons since he'd turned thirty-five.

"Not since he's been DJ," Chuck explained.

"You're a DJ? Since when?"

Bruce ignored the question, having reached for his duffle bag and begun busily rooting through it.

"Two months ago," again Chuck volunteered the information, moving around to the driver's side.

"So you're not in programming anymore?" Ike asked. Ike was a man who looked like he belonged in the bush. He was solid, with curly hair and a bushy beard that had become silver.

Bruce pretended dismay as he stood up wearing a CHUM baseball cap. "You mean none of you guys have heard me on the air?"

"Nope." Ike shook his head and Tim shrugged.

"What station did you say you were on?" Archie, Ike's brother-in-law, leaned out from Ike's truck, to look straight at Bruce with his bright white cap. Archie, who *was* fat and out of shape—he was a truck driver, hadn't moved since he and Ike had pulled in, except to open a can of beer from out of the back of the truck and start drinking it.

"CHUM," Bruce answered before he realized it was a tease.

"CHUM? *I* don't listen to CHUM. Do *you* listen to CHUM?"

"Never. Do you?"

Chuck grinned as he stood up and then walked around to return the tire gauge to the glove compartment of Bruce's truck.

"CHUM? You gotta be kidding. Who'd wanna listen to CHUM?" They all burst out laughing.

"That's it. You can *all* ride with Ike! No one's coming in my truck!" Bruce slammed the back of his truck shut, thrust out his chest like a peacock, then burst into laughter himself.

Just then, Smithy finally came out his front door, carrying a cooler and a box of food. "So who's going with who?" he asked, as he came down his steps to the trucks.

Tim groaned.

"Look, I don't care," Ike spoke up and swung around, getting ready to drive. "Archie can come with me."

Smithy put the stuff he was carrying into Ike's open truck and then closed the door.

"And in the interests of size and space, why don't you go with them," Chuck asked Tim, "and Smithy and me'll go with Bruce."

"Fine with me," Tim said. He walked over to Archie's side, then changed his mind. Anticipating him, Ike swung down to let him in on his side.

"Chuck, you *did* put the beer in the back, yeah?" Bruce asked.

"Yeah, it's there."

Smithy climbed into the front of Bruce's truck, and Chuck got in behind him. Ike and Bruce confirmed the tradition with each other—"The Petrocan on Eleven?"—then climbed into their drivers' seats and started their trucks.

They were headed to Bruce's cabin, which was tucked in the bush between two little towns and Algonquin Park in what was called 'The Near North'. The drive wasn't all that long, usually three, three and a half, four hours at the most. But sitting three in front could be tight, and the stop was always a welcome chance to stretch. Besides, 'gasoline alley' on the outskirts of Orillia had the cheapest gas in all of Ontario.

They backed out of Smithy's driveway, and headed up toward Eglinton. From there they caught the Allan Expressway to the 401.

Sure enough, as soon as they hit the 401, Archie dozed off.

"How can he be a truck driver?" Tim asked Ike. "Doesn't he fall asleep at the wheel?"

"I guess not," Ike answered. "Actually, I think he's got a fifteen-year record of no accidents."

"Amazing."

Though he was a high school shop teacher in the city now, Ike did in fact grow up in the bush. He was a basic kind of guy—strong, with lots of opinions but not a whole lot of words. He reached down to loosen the laces on his boots a bit, then settled in for the drive.

Tim might've liked a bit of conversation but he didn't mind its absence either. He wasn't one of those runners who plugged into a headset; his mind could amuse itself for hours at a stretch. He tried to get comfortable against Archie's mass to give a bit of room to Ike.

When they stopped at the Petrocan, it was clear that the ambience in Bruce's truck was a bit different. Bruce had already gassed up, and the three of them were standing by his truck telling jokes.

Smithy held out his right hand. "Why can't you masturbate with this hand?" he asked.

Chuck and Bruce both shook their heads. "I don't know, why?" Chuck asked.

"Cuz it's *mine!*" Smithy shouted, pulling his hand back possessively. He danced around, laughing, and with his lanky body he looked like a hysterical Donald Sutherland in a M.A.S.H. out-take.

"How many psychiatrists does it take to change a light bulb?" he asked.

"I don't know, how many?" Tim had joined them, while Ike filled up his truck and Archie went in to buy something to eat.

"One, but the light bulb has to really *want* to change." Smithy was beside himself by this time laughing at his own jokes. The others were laughing too—partly at Smithy and partly at his jokes. Not for the first time, Bruce wondered just how good a psychologist Smithy really was. He had been what's called an 'industrial psychologist' for about twelve years, mostly measuring mental health in the workplace, on a contractual freelance basis. But he'd mentioned he was thinking about applying for some position with the Ministry of Health.

"I got another one, listen. What do you call a crazy person who gets lost in the snow?"

Even before anyone could say 'I don't know, what?' Smithy blurted out loudly enough for everyone at the station to hear, "A frosted flake!" Bruce and Chuck stuffed him back into their truck, and Tim rejoined Ike and Archie who were by now ready to carry on.

In another hour and a half they reached Sundridge, which was sort of halfway between Huntsville and North Bay. They turned off the highway, drove along Main Street and Lake Bernard, then drove out of town along what was informally called Forest Lake Road. They drove past the dump onto a dirt road, past the township office, past the house with two horses and a goat. Forest Lake Road became Paisley Lake Road, and they kept driving. Past Paisley Lake. Past Butterfield Lake. Then into the bush on an old logging road. A couple miles later they came to Bruce's cabin.

It was around ten o'clock by this time and there was no moon, so they stumbled around in the dark for a bit until Bruce unlocked the cabin door and lit a few kerosene lamps. The cabin really *was* a cabin—nothing fancy, nothing very finished. Bruce had built it himself several years ago for probably no more than ten thousand.

There was no need to decide who would do what. Everyone did what they always did. Ike got the water jugs from inside the cabin and made his way to the nearby spring, while Bruce got a fire going in the woodstove. Smithy found a flashlight and headed off to the outhouse. The others brought in all their stuff from the trucks. Chuck put the food and beer into the fridge outside; without hydro it acted more like a thermos than a fridge, but at least it kept the food from the animals. When Ike returned, he filled a kettle with water and set it on the woodstove. Tim and Archie did whatever else needed to be done.

Tired, and knowing they'd be getting up at five for the hunt the next morning, they settled in fairly quickly. Since it was Bruce's place, he took the main bed in the only bedroom. They tossed for the spare bed—Tim got it this year. Ike claimed the couch. Chuck got the pull-out cot from the closet, and Smithy and Archie cleared the floor in front of the woodstove.

"Five o'clock?" Tim checked, and getting nods all round, he set his fancy wristwatch. It not only had an alarm; it had a stopwatch.

After a few minutes, the kerosene lamps were put out and everything was dark and still and quiet. Ike was reminded of his childhood. Then of the seven years he had left before early retirement. He intended to move back up north and stay there. It wasn't that he disliked teaching; it's just that the city was, well, the city. If, fifteen years ago, he could've gotten a job up at the high school in Mattawa or even North Bay, he would've. But fifteen years ago only Toronto was hiring.

Archie snored. A few of the others groaned and Tim called out, "who's beside Archie?"

"I am." That was Smithy.

"Well, give him a good swift kick, will ya?"

Smithy nudged Archie, and he stopped. Silence again.

"Why did the chicken cross to the other side of the road?" Everyone groaned.

"He doesn't know, but he's in analysis to find out." Smithy laughed infectiously.

"Smithy?"

"Yes, Bruce?"

"Go the fuck to sleep."

"Yes, Bruce."

At five o'clock, Tim's watch began to beep and the men began to wake up, get up, and wash up, in various stages. Bruce lit the lamps and put a couple more chunks of wood into the stove to take out the October chill.

His wood pile was behind the cabin on the way from the outhouse. Someone had put a huge pot of water on the stove a few hours before so there was hot water for washing. Smithy filled a kettle and put it on to boil for coffee. Chuck got some mugs out of the cupboard and found a jar of coffee in one of the boxes of food Tim had brought in from the fridge.

"I brought some of those little juice cartons if anyone wants juice instead of coffee," Tim offered, rummaging in the food box.

"How 'bout in addition to?" Chuck reached out his hand to accept one.

Most of the guys had by now gathered around the woodstove, sitting on various chairs and the single couch that filled the so-called living room.

"Well, look at this!" Chuck whistled. He was staring at Archie, who had just appeared in the bedroom doorway all decked out in what was clearly a brand new outfit: grey-green camouflage pants, matching t-shirt, jacket, and hat, and heavy boots.

He grinned, "Well, you guys all take this hunting thing so seriously, thought I'd give it a try." He turned sideways to get through the doorway, then, to great cheering and whistling, he sashayed to a pose in front of the woodstove. Ike was surprised to see Archie like this. Maybe he was still half asleep.

The others were not quite so dressed up for the occasion. Tim had changed his jeans for sweatpants, Bruce and Chuck wore the standard fare, straight out of Sportsman magazine, and Smithy—well—it looked like Smithy's wife had dressed him. Out of the Sears catalogue. And Ike—as always, Ike had on that well-worn brown jacket that looked like he grew up in it. Probably did. It was warm. It was waterproof. And it was full of pockets.

"All right," Bruce said, "let's get down to business." He got the deck of cards from a cupboard in the kitchen. Same deck as every year. They gathered around and cleared the up-ended chunk of log that served as an end table. He shuffled and then dealt. Five, six, jack, three, ten, queen.

"Ike, you're it!" Bruce pointed to the queen. They all cheered.

"All right!" Chuck slapped him on the back. "This year's hunt is gonna be gooood!" He finished his coffee, grabbed his green checked jacket and went outside.

"Way to go, Ike," Archie heaved himself up and headed outside.

"Yeah, this is gonna be great!" Smithy, like the others, was excited about the challenge.

Ike had never been hunter before. Every year it was someone else. This year it was him. He smiled. Couldn't conceal his delight.

Once they had all gathered outside, Ike looked at his watch. "Everyone got five-forty-two? Okay, I'll start at six. Hunt's over at nine."

"Ooh, an extra three minutes this year! Thank you, Ike!" Tim checked his watch.

"Everyone back at nine-thirty?" Ike asked. They all grunted assent.

"Everyone got their number?" They nodded. They were ready.

"Okay," Ike said, then couldn't resist adding with a glint, "See you all later". He went back into the cabin, and the others took off.

He sat on a chair, both hands around his coffee mug, thinking about what he was about to do. No one had ever gotten five before. He could. And this year, he would.

Six o'clock. He put a six-pack into his beaten-up knapsack and headed out. He decided to follow the path that headed north first. It was a brisk day, cooler than other years. But it would be clear. The dew was drying and soon the forest would be bright. He remembered the year it was raining. What a mess! What was the catch that year, two? He remembered Chuck, Bruce, and Tim had really gotten into it. They had piled into Bruce's truck after breakfast, completely covered with mud and oozing with every step, and drove back into town, hoping to use the showers at the motel. The owner took one look at them and told them to go jump in the lake. And so they did. All three of them. In the middle of October. Turkeys.

After about half an hour of travelling, Ike heard a noise. He stopped. Nothing. He started walking again. There on his left. Steps? Yes, definitely steps. He looked—saw nothing. He took off his knapsack, carefully laid it down on the ground, then left the path. All of a sudden someone made a run for it maybe twenty or thirty yards ahead of him. He shouted out, "I got you!"

"Oh yeah?" Chuck's voice. "What's my number?" he taunted.

"Just a minute and I'll tell you!" Ike took a few more steps and heard a rustle in response ahead of him. He picked up a few rocks and tossed them to his right. The rustle moved to the left. He started toward it on a diagonal this time. Ever so slowly. Stepping ever so carefully. He threw a few more rocks to his right. The rustle moved closer. But damn it, he couldn't see a thing, the bush was so thick here. He walked further on. Not a sound.

Chuck was crouched in the undergrowth, on his hands and knees staring out to the right. Ike was good. He couldn't hear his steps anymore, but he knew he was coming. He felt him. He stared, but couldn't see anything but trees and brush. It was so quiet.

"Forty-nine."

Chuck swung around to see Ike grinning directly at him. He looked at the pinny he was wearing, like the ones they used in high school playing basketball in phys-ed class, as if he couldn't believe that the number sewn on the frayed cotton square was forty-nine. He looked back to the right, pointing, and then when he realized what Ike had done he cried out, "Why you old bugger!"

He scrambled up as if to make a run for it. Useless, since Ike knew his number, but at least he could keep his pinny. But Ike was expecting it. He lunged for him and soon the two were hollering on the ground, laughing, as Ike wrestled his pinny off him. Chuck kneeled, stripped of his number, now dangling from Ike's belt loop.

"Shit," he said, then got up and started to head back down the path toward the cabin. It was only six-thirty. Ike grinned and went back to the path to get his knapsack, then headed a bit further north up the path. He felt the swing of number forty-nine against his thigh and smiled again. The day was warming up just a touch. After ten or fifteen minutes, he came to the creek. He followed it east for a bit till it met with the other path. He looked around. Nothing. The soft earth by the creek had no footprints. The creek itself was clear, the bed undisturbed. He heard the occasional bird. He started off down the path. The forest was so beautiful like this. Silent. and full. When he came to the fork, he took the left on impulse. After another fifteen minutes, another fork. Geez, he wouldn't have time to follow them all. Left again on a hunch. He walked quickly but carefully. Listening, looking, trying even to smell—but nothing. Nothing. He kept going, intending to take the next left too because it circled back to the main path. Still looking, noticing everything.

All of a sudden, he stopped, shot his pointing finger upward, and bellowed, "Smithy!" He looked up to see Smithy almost fall out of the tree. "Fourteen!"

Smithy recovered his footing and scrambled down, not unlike an adolescent ape. Ike was waiting at the bottom, his hand outstretched, grinning.

"How the hell?" Smithy muttered as he took off his number.

Ike pointed to the bark on the tree about three feet up. It was scraped, and there was a small black scuff mark.

"That's no deer," he said smugly, still grinning.

"Well, you clever son of a bitch." Smithy handed Ike his number for this year's hunt, number fourteen.

They walked together back to the main path. Once there, Smithy headed down toward the cabin. Ike decided to go back up towards the creek. It was close to seven-thirty. It was about half an hour to the bend. Well, might as well. Who knows what might be found on the way.

He got to the bend in twenty-five minutes. He looked around, trying to decide. Yes. Here would do it. He took the six-pack out of his knapsack, walked a bit off the path at the peak of the bend, and tossed it half under some bushes. Then he went back a bit to climb a dense but tall tree he'd noticed just around the bend. Perfect, he said to himself as he perched rather comfortably with a good view of the six-pack, but out of sight of the path to it.

He waited ten minutes. Twenty minutes. He looked at his watch. Damn. Eight-fifteen. He'd *have* to be coming down soon.

At eight-seventeen, he heard him. Slow cautious steps. He waited. The steps got closer, then slower— He saw it. Bruce came into view. This was too easy, Ike chuckled to himself. But he couldn't make out his number yet. Bruce looked around, puzzled. He looked at the trail behind him, then peered once more into the bush on his left, on his right. He stepped closer, to the six-pack, to Ike. He bent down to the six-pack. Just as soon as he had one in his hand, he heard Ike's voice, "That Bud's for you ..."

Instantly he realized what had happened. "Fuck!" he cried out and threw the can to the ground. "That wasn't fair!" He looked around to locate the still singing voice. "This was a trap! I was baited!" he cried with indignation. Ike was taking his time climbing down the tree, still singing. "You old buzzard!" Bruce was still cursing. He couldn't believe he'd gotten suckered in like that.

Ike walked out of the bush, and across the path, to where Bruce was stamping and slapping a tree here and there. He picked up the can Bruce had tossed and opened it. It sprayed all over Bruce, like a mad dog being hosed down. Ike then held it out to him and with his other hand waited for the pinny. They traded. Bruce took a few slugs from the can and started laughing. "This was a good one, ol' boy." He took a few more gulps then said, "What I can't figure is how did you know to bait me *here?*"

Ike grinned. "Smithy needed someone to boost him into the tree. He's long, but he's not that long."

Bruce shook his head in wonderment.

Ike looked at his watch. Eight-thirty. Only half an hour left. And he'd gotten only three. Time to head back or the three he'd gotten wouldn't even count. He left Bruce with the beer and started at a trot back down to the cabin. He passed no one, nothing, on the way. Not one tell-tale crow flying overhead even. Damn. Where could they be? Archie and Tim, they were the two that were left. Where would they go?

He stood outside the cabin. The sun was shining brightly now. What could he do in two minutes? Even so, he wasn't about to quit yet. He knew these guys. They'd all been buddies for years. In fact, the five of them helped Bruce build this cabin. He knew everything about them. What they drank, what they ate, their sore spots, their good points, their hobbies, their habits—aha. He walked over to the truck. I don't believe it, he thought, but it's worth a try. He opened the passenger door. And the noise startled Archie from his doze.

"Twenty-two," Ike said as he looked at his watch and walked to the cabin. Archie rubbed his eyes and started to move his cramped legs.

Ike walked into the cabin. Smithy and Chuck were sitting on the couch in front of the woodstove, eyes on their watches. It was nine o'clock sharp.

"Two?" Chuck asked.

"Three," Bruce corrected as he appeared in the doorway and raised his can of beer to Ike.

"No, four," Ike said as Archie lumbered in and, half sleep-blind, put his pinny into Ike's outstretched hand.

"Coffee," Archie mumbled, squinting at their cups.

"Where was he?" Bruce asked.

"In the truck," Ike answered.

"No," Smithy said in disbelief.

"Yeah."

"He was in the truck all this time?" Chuck asked.

"Sleeping like a babe."

"Coffee," Archie was rattling in the kitchen for the jar of coffee.

"You guys didn't give me any coffee this morning," he whined.

"Archie, it *is* morning," Smithy answered.

Archie paused. "Then when was before?"

"So where's Tim?" Bruce asked.

"Yeah, anyone seen Tim?" Smithy echoed.

"Nope. He split. Took off up the north path—haven't seen him since," Chuck answered.

"Well, he's still got time. Fifteen minutes yet," Bruce answered.

"Yeah, but if he doesn't make it, Ike here will be the first to get five!" Smithy slapped him on the back.

"So, who's making breakfast?" Archie had gotten himself a cup of coffee and had made his way into a chair, an old upholstered green thing with broken springs.

"Yeah, breakfast!" Smithy got up and headed out to the fridge. Bruce got a couple fry pans from where they were hanging on nails on the wall. He rinsed them out while Chuck scrounged for bowls and various utensils. Ike looked at his watch and opened the door to look out. Nothing.

"So what's it like being a DJ?" Smithy asked Bruce while he chopped up a bunch of stuff.

"Yeah, what station did you say you worked for?" Archie had come a bit to life.

"Geez, why don't you talk to Chuck about his job instead?"

"Chuck, you got a job? I thought you were still on unemployment," Smithy turned from cracking eggs.

"I am. Bruce's just getting back at me for telling you about his new 'career'."

"Any luck looking yet?" Archie asked from his chair.

"No, not really," Chuck answered. He stood by Bruce and looked over Smithy's shoulder. "Did he put enough salt in?"

"I don't think he's put any salt in yet."

"Smithy, you are going to put salt in this time, aren't you?"

It began to look like a 'Three Stooges' scene. Smithy pointed to one bowl. "That one gets salt. Here." He handed them the salt shaker. "This one's mine," he hugged the other bowl to his chest.

"It's nine-twenty-six," Archie spoke up. Ike was still hovering by the door, opening it every now and then.

"I bet he doesn't make it," Bruce said.

"You got it," Chuck replied. "Twenty bucks."

"Twenty and a case of two-four," Bruce upped the wager.

"You're on."

"Are you guys putting any cheese in that stuff?" Archie called out.

"No," Smithy called back. "Just salt."

"Salt's good," Archie approved.

Smithy put the pans on the stove and covered them. He looked at his watch. "Nine-twenty-nine and counting".

They all got on their feet and gathered in the center of the room, patting Ike on the back, counting down in unison.

"Ten—nine—eight—seven—"

Suddenly the door opened. Tim hung on the frame. Panting. Sweating. And staring at his watch.

"Nine-twenty-nine-fifty-four, right? I made it?" He looked up at the others.

"Where the hell have you been?" Bruce asked.

Tim staggered in and collapsed on the couch. He smiled wanly. "Out."

Chuck then thought of it. "I bet he went to the ridge."

"You went to the ridge?" Smithy asked, wide-eyed.

Tim nodded, heaving a little less now.

"But that's almost ten miles away," Bruce said.

"Then straight up and straight down," Tim gasped.

"You went to the *top* of the ridge?" Smithy asked. "And back? In three hours?"

"Ike, you're a clever bastard. I know that," Tim said then, out of breath but clearly. "I figured the only way to beat you was to outrun you."

"You got *that* right," the others muttered and nodded.

"Say, isn't the ridge out of bounds?" Bruce mentioned casually.

"Yeah, didn't we decide that we could go only as far as the bottom?" Chuck supported him.

"What? We didn't decide that." Tim staggered to his feet, appalled. "When did we say that?" His pulse started to race again. "No one told *me!*" he pleaded to Ike.

Ike hesitated for just a moment, then said, "No, they're just playing with you. You made it," he reached out to shake his hand, "fair and square."

"So, let's get on with the show, shall we?" Archie heaved himself out of the chair.

Ike complied, unfastening the four pinnies from his belt loop. Bruce, Chuck, Smithy, Archie, and Tim cheered and whistled then, as he spiked the bunch of four into the wall next to the other clumps of twos, threes, and one other four. He pulled out his jack-knife and carved his name and the year underneath.

They raised their beer or coffee or whatever in a toast to this year's hunt. Then sat down to eat breakfast.

"Next year," Bruce announced, "I'm gonna bring a pair of stilts, with moose legs tied onto them."

"Yeah? And next year *I'm* gonna run to the ridge and back," Archie said, expecting the laughter he got as he reached for another helping.

"Next year," Smithy offered, "I'm going to wear my shoes backwards."

"That's great, Smithy," Chuck said to him, "because then your feet will match your head." More laughter, and another toast.

War Heroes

Phan Ling completed the one remaining calculation, neatly printed '47.12' onto the large sheet fixed on her drafting table, then carefully set down her pencil. She stretched, leaned back with her arms crossed behind her head, and looked out the window of her fifth floor office. The usual feeling of triumph—or at least satisfaction—was not forthcoming. She was puzzled: she had been working on this assignment for months.

Well, she realized, she hadn't been too excited about it in the first place. It was the design of a fission trigger which would initiate the fusion reaction of a thermonuclear weapon. But, she knew she couldn't pick and choose her assignments—no one in R and D could. No one in *any* department could. You can't just accept parts of your job, the stuff you liked, and refuse the rest. A company can't function if it can't trust its employees to do what they were asked to do—she knew that. She understood that.

And it wasn't as if all of her assignments had to do with nuclear weapons. In fact, this was the first. She knew the company itself wasn't comfortable with this particular contract—but, well, it had saved them from bankruptcy.

No. generally speaking, she liked her job, she liked the challenge of her work. So she wasn't about to get radical and become an activist over this one assignment. It wasn't in her nature. It wasn't in her background. When her parents' parents became frustrated at the lack of opportunity at home for a university education for their children, they didn't take to the streets shouting and waving banners, demanding more universities, and condemning the government's complacency with the rampant under-the-table bribery that went on for the few spaces at the existing universities. They simply sold a family heirloom, withdrew their savings, and sent their youngest and brightest here, to Canada. They simply saw an alternative and quietly took it.

Then when her own parents discovered the persistent disadvantage of their poorly spoken English, they didn't cry 'discrimination!' and call for meetings with the student unions, they just decided to switch majors, from anthropology and psychology to engineering and physics, fields in which the disadvantage would be minimalized. Like them, Phan believed that you could get what you more or less wanted *within* the confines of laws and regulations. with a little intelligence and a lot of hard work.

That's why the news this morning—ah! There's the reason! She had heard on the news this morning that the arms talk had failed. *That* was why she didn't feel very good about her successfully completed assignment. By themselves, one or the other wouldn't have upset her. But timing can create such a juxtaposition—

Of course it wasn't the first arms talk. And it wasn't the first arms talk that had failed. The U.S. had begun testing in 1945. The Soviet Union, in '49, and the UK, in '52, Six years later, thirteen years after the atomic bomb, negotiations began for a ban on testing. The three countries actually agreed then to stop it, for two years. But before those two years were over, the U.S. walked out on further negotiations. France began testing in 1960, the USSR and the U.S. resumed in 1961. By that time, the Intercontinental Bomber, the hydrogen bomb, the Intercontinental Ballistic Missile, the man-made satellite in orbit for targeting and surveillance, and the submarine launched ballistic missile had been successfully developed.

Over the next fifteen or sixteen years, a mere four treaties were established. All were limited in scope, all were 'partial'. Then in 1977, the three countries got together again and talked about a comprehensive test ban treaty; two years later, the U.S. and the USSR signed the Strategic Arms Limitation Agreement, the one known as Salt II, but the U.S. Senate didn't ratify it, and in 1980 the U.S. refused to continue negotiations. In 1985, the USSR declared a unilateral moratorium on nuclear testing; they even extended it four times, until 1987. But no one else joined in; and they started testing again. In the meantime, the multiple warhead, the Antiballistic Missile, the Multiple Independent Targeted Warhead, and long range cruise missiles had been developed. And testing was taking place in China and India as well.

She began to lose track then as every talk became enmeshed in a complex web of ifs, ands, and buts. How many SS-20s equal how many Pershing IIs? Then denials and declarations began that put even 'the facts' in question. Maybe the U.S. didn't discontinue negotiations, maybe the USSR didn't maintain a moratorium. Were the warheads withdrawn as promised? Did the freeze occur at the level agreed to?

Who would ever know what had happened in the past—certainly the present state of affairs was muddy. And the future was—well, invisible. Were egos blocking the vision? Was it that too much was invested to turn back now? She didn't know why the talks had failed.

She knew only that negotiations weren't working. She thought for a moment, then she picked up her pencil, erased '47.12', and printed '47.22'. Now the triggers wouldn't work either. She stretched and leaned back in her chair again—smiling with pride at a job well done.

Karl Nyovsky worked in a place that looked like an old military base, except that it had shiny barn-like buildings. It was in fact an industrial facility, a metalworking factory. The metal used was plutonium. The plutonium was melted, then poured through a tantalm funnel in to a graphite mold. The resulting ingots came down the line to Karl, to be machined into the proper shape. He was a tool-and-die maker by trade. Here he made nuclear triggers.

Almost every factory worker knew someone who had lost a finger somehow somewhere, and Karl was no exception. Yes, he was very aware of accidents; in fact if he had another skill, he'd find another job. However, from behind a stainless steel enclosure, with lead glass windows, lead shielding, and lead oxide in the rubber gloves he wore, Karl wasn't thinking of losing a finger.

He was thinking of accidents he'd read about. Three-Mile Island and Chernobyl. (In fact, if the money weren't so good, he'd find another job.) But Karl didn't read just the *Sun* or the *Star* or the *Globe*. He also read the other newspapers, the small alternative, almost underground, newsletters and pamphlets that came his way, sometimes by subscription, sometimes by random outreach. It was a habit he had brought with him from home.

So as he worked, Karl was also thinking of the B-52 carrying four nuclear bombs that crashed in Greenland in 1968, spreading 16 kg of plutonium over acres and acres of tundra. More than 230,000 cubic feet of ice and debris were scraped up and disposed. Where, Karl wondered, as he lined up the next ingot, where was it disposed to? He also thought of the Russian airplane carrying a nuclear weapon that crashed in the Sea of Japan. He thought of the U.S. subs carrying nuclear missiles that have collided with Russian ships, the *George Washington* that ran right into a Japanese ship back in '81, and the *Scorpion* and the *Thresher*, two nuclear attack submarines that just sank into the ocean and no one knows why. He checked the setting readouts above the four knobs, '1.18', '47.22', '15.6', and '7.64', and thought of the nuclear weapon that fell out of a strategic bomber in the late '70s and landed in Carolina in a swamp. He thought of the failure in 1979 of a 46¢ computer part that produced a false signal showing Russian missiles on the way to the U.S., and of the missile that was accidentally fired from Arkansas in '81 because a mechanic dropped a wrench. Oh yes, he knew, accidents happen, people make mistakes.

The chance of a nuclear war starting by accident was, to his mind, phenomenal. He thought of the four plutonium bombs dropped on Spain by mistake—fortunately they didn't explode. He thought of the crash in '61 of a plane carrying a 24 megaton bomb over North Carolina—on impact, five of the six interlocking mechanisms on the bomb failed, so that only one switch prevented an explosion equivalent to 1,000 Nagasakis. One switch had made the difference. Chances are, he thought, adjusting the precision controls, this one will also be fired by mistake. He turned one of the knobs just a few more degrees. But chances are, he smiled, it won't go off.

Claude Tremblay was lying awake in bed at 5:00 a.m. He was on his back, staring at the ceiling. He was trying to decide whether or not to call in sick.

He was scheduled for what the guys called a 'nuke run'. Transporting something or other—they never knew just what—in those canisters marked with that radioactive symbol, always to or from some military base. The runs paid sometimes five times a regular run—which is why a lot of guys put in special requests for them. But for exactly the same reason they paid so much, a lot of guys didn't like them—the personal risk. What happened if your rig got in an accident? Well, no one really knew for sure—they said it was safe enough and talked a lot about the construction of the canisters—but well, Claude didn't always believe what he was told.

However, that wasn't what was really bothering him. Every time he saw one of those symbols, he saw people running, on fire, their skin hanging in strips. He saw schools, hospitals, buildings of all kinds, blasted to bits, the steel, concrete, and glass shards flying into people's bodies. He saw people lying everywhere injured, dying. He saw others walk by, unable to help, but with nowhere to go.

He saw people with radiation sickness, throwing up, their hair falling out, just waiting to die. He saw hundreds of dull and empty eyes, suffering acute stress, bereavement, and depression. He saw people living in a cold and barren wasteland, desperate with survival instinct, looting and killing for a bottle of water, a can of beans. He saw the survivors sprouting cancers, gradually malfunctioning.

When he told the guys once, they looked at him like he was some kind of wimp. It was okay to consider the risk to yourself, but it wasn't cool to think about others. He didn't understand. Then some new guy got on his high horse and refused all nuke runs, saying it was our duty to our children to resist, etc., etc. Claude tried to figure it—duty was okay but care wasn't? It was okay to care about others only if the others were your kids? Well, if your kids are merely extensions of your self, he saw their logic in that—he noticed that a lot of people suddenly became concerned citizens when they became parents. The new guy was suspended—they were trying to decide if they could fire him.

Claude didn't want to be suspended too—or fired. He liked— well, yeah, he liked his job: he liked being in the driver's seat, he was his own boss more or less, he made his own decisions—didn't have to ask no floor super if he could go to the can. The bed creaked as he shifted his position. Well then be your own boss, *make* your own decisions.

Still—what's one trip? He stared at the ceiling. and saw that damn symbol. And then saw again all the people— what he saw made him sick. He picked up the phone.

Alabua Achebe was pacing outside the assembly building at the base, waiting anxiously for the truck. She looked again toward the gate. It was an hour and a half late. Where was the damn thing? She had to have the trigger installed by five o'clock today.

Tons of money poured into this whole business and still it's a mess! (It was income tax time and money was uppermost in her mind.) Fifteen percent of my taxes go to the Department of Defence, she thought, fifteen percent! She had been thinking about withholding that fifteen percent. Redirecting it to the Peace Tax Fund. Well half of it anyway. She wasn't one of the naive who were *totally* anti-military. She wouldn't be here if she were. No. Alabua admired much of what the military did. She had joined mainly for the educational opportunities and for the peace-keeping and rescue aspects of the job. But then she was transferred. And transferred again. As Junior personnel it was hard to say no because who knew then if you'd ever see a raise or a promotion again. But it was hard as senior personnel too because the expectations of loyalty were so great. And of course the transfers were always temporary. Yet with each transfer, she became a little more disillusioned. But what was she to do. Just say no? Quit? Walk away from a job that had given her a university degree, not to mention a great dental/medical plan, life and disability insurance, and a fantastic pension to boot? It had occurred to her. It had become harder and harder to defend against the 'little boys with big toys' accusation of her non-military friends. And the money, the expense, was certainly one part of it. She discovered that the old joke about $20 for a manually-operable torque device—a screwdriver—was true. She always wondered where the difference between $20 and $4.99 went. Not into *her* pocket. (Though she had no complaints.) In the States, the profits made by arms manufacturers exceed those made in civilian industry by twenty to thirty percent. It was something to think about. At the edge of the building she turned with impatience and walked the other way.

So was fifteen percent. And she realized that that didn't include things like the $13 million subsidy the federal government had given to

Litton to manufacture the guidance system for the cruise missile. That $13 million came out of the other 85% of my taxes, she figured. How many more such subsidies were there?

No one had been charged or sent to jail for redirecting taxes, as long as the test case, the one with Dr. Prior, was unsettled. But as soon as she lost, people were being hauled in left, right, and center, to pay for their conscientious objection. More and more every year.

It was no wonder, Alabua thought, as she turned and walked back again. The military industry produces fewer jobs per dollar than any other sector, everyone knew that by now. It created 75 jobs where construction created 100, health care 138, and education 187. And what had she read the other day? That the global arms race was costing the world $2 million a minute? (It was expensive to go nuclear—especially when you buy 25,000 warheads where 200 would do—she knew the requirements for deterrence.) And that to provide adequate food, clean water, education, health care, and housing for everyone on the planet would cost $17 billion a year—that's, she turned again as she did the arithmetic, that's a little over six days: less than one week, one week's military spending out of fifty-two, would take care of the world's basic needs. She stopped. It was incredible. What are we, she wondered, crazy? She turned slowly and started walking again, toward the gate. and through it.

Bill Lancaster set his pencil and management textbook onto the bare table in front of him—he was half-way through chapter nine. He looked at the clock—lots of time yet. He yawned and glanced around. This was why he liked this assignment, why he had volunteered for missile duty. Twenty-four hours in a capsule with virtually dick-all to do. At the rate he was going, he'd have his MBA by winter, fall maybe. He stood up to stretch and walked around checking the many indicator meters. A lot of guys brought correspondence coursework with them. Except Fisco—she moonlighted as an accountant and brought her clients' books to work on. And Dubb—he didn't bring anything—and usually fell asleep after eight or ten hours. He finished his check, everything was as it should be. He turned back to chapter nine, fiddling absently with the 'combat' pin on the lapel of his neatly pressed uniform.

After a few hours, he took another break before launching into the chapter's questions. It was six o'clock, the controls would be switched to missile two now, the one with the newly installed trigger. He poured himself a cup of coffee, offered one to his partner in the adjoining capsule, then sat down to go through his mail—one could not live on coursework alone.

A few bills he tucked inside his wallet. A letter from his foster-child in Peru he read with some delight and put into his pocket—it would get taped to his fridge. Some junk mail—a record club offer he *could* refuse, a plea from the cancer society, and something from an anti-nuclear group. He flung that last one onto the table. He was sure they had a separate mailing list, some kind of hit list, of all DND employees.

Yes he knew that between the soot and dust from the explosion that would darken the planet and absorb the heat, causing the surface temperature to decrease, and the radioactive fallout that would contaminate soil and water wherever it drifted—yes one thing leads to another, the face of the earth would be changed: it would no longer sustain life as we know it. Yes he knew that. It was so well-publicized, you'd have to be an idiot not to know. Or a psychopath—was that the name for people who blocked out certain aspects of reality?

But that would never happen, didn't they know that? This was all a charade, a scare tactic. That's what this country's military strategy was based on: *threat*, the *potential* for devastating attack or retaliation. And even though it was the mere threat that was important, it couldn't be an empty threat, they had to actually have all the missiles they said they did. Granted, it wasn't the best military strategy in the world, but a battlefield of nuclear weapons wasn't your best military scenario either. You had to deal with the facts, and the fact was nuclear weapons existed, but it would never happen.

And if it did—well—he'd do as he'd been trained, he'd follow orders, he'd act— No, he'd *react*. He was like a rat: the light goes on, you do a little trick, and you get a pellet. He glanced at the envelope from the nuclear group. No, you get killed. It wasn't the best military strategy in the world.

Suddenly the alarm in the capsule went off. Bill jumped to the control panel, seeing the red light flashing. He began to go through his routine: one—off, yes; two—on, yes; three—over ten, yes; four—switch up, yes; five—key turn five—key turn—no.

Going Shopping

Adelaide carried the pot of tea from the counter to the little kitchen table. The table was already set from the night before: a cup and saucer on either side, next to a bread plate and knife. The butter dish was in the center, beside the empty spot where she now put the teapot. It was good china, a wedding gift, forty years old. It had lasted longer than Albert.

Greta came out of the second bedroom and entered the kitchen of their small apartment.

"Good morning, Adelaide!" she said brightly, opening the fridge. She always got the little jars of jam out, and added the cream to the cream-and-sugar beside the teapot.

"Good morning. Sleep well?" Adelaide asked.

"Oh, you know for me it's not the sleeping that's a problem, it's the getting up out of bed that bothers me."

Adelaide did know that. And today was Saturday. Shopping day.

"Is it too bad to go shopping today? We can always—"

"Oh no! I can certainly go shopping! The day these old bones can't go shopping Adelaide, why that's the day I'll just roll over and die."

They both smiled. Greta got the loaf of bread out of the breadbox, and put two slices into the toaster. She then sat across from Adelaide.

"I wonder what Woolworth's has on sale today," Adelaide said with devilish glee in her eyes.

"Now, Adelaide, don't you start. We'll just have to wait and see." Greta followed the script. She peeked into the teapot. "It's fine for you, I think," she said to Adelaide, who liked her tea a little less strong than Greta.

Adelaide peeked too and then poured herself a cup. The toast popped up and Greta started to get out of her chair.

"I'll get it, dear, you stay put." Adelaide flitted from her chair to the kitchen counter. She was the smaller of the two and had an air of fragility whereas Greta appeared solid. But Greta's body seemed to have lost its shock absorbers, whereas Adelaide's was still springy. And so, in fact, Greta was the one more liable to break. And she was heavier. But then again, she was also stronger— So it was hard to say, really.

Adelaide put a plate with two pieces of toast on it in the center of the table, then sat down. Each took a piece onto her bread plate then paused, deciding.

They looked at each other as if this was some sort of paper-rock-and-scissors game. Then Greta quickly reached out for the raspberry jam, and Adelaide snatched the apricot marmalade. They laughed at their own silliness. The grape jelly and the pear-pineapple stood unchosen.

"It looks like it's going to be a sunny day," Adelaide commented.

"Yes, though it's still early morning. It's got time to change its mind."

"Do you think that new store—that new ice cream store—what's its name? One of those silly hyphenated—Baskin-Rubens?"

"Baskin-Robbins," Greta knew it.

"Yes that's it, Baskin-Robbins. Do you think it will be open today?"

"I don't know. Maybe—"

"Can you imagine?" Adelaide said. "Thirty-one flavours!"

They finished their toast and tea after a few moments, then Adelaide announced with excitement. "All right, time to get down to business. Shall I get the paper or will you?" Greta didn't answer. She was staring out of the window, lost. "Greta?"

Greta looked at Adelaide then, "Why don't we both go?"

"Both?" Adelaide was surprised. "Why?"

"Well, I've been thinking," Greta looked out the window again. "You know that new young lady who's just moved in two doors down?"

"Yes ..."

"Well, she lives alone as far as I can tell," she looked at Adelaide's generous blue eyes, "and I don't think anyone's said so much as hello to her." She stopped, cautiously. "Why don't we invite her along with us today?" She wasn't sure how Adelaide would take this. Going shopping had always been a 'just the two of them' thing.

"Why Greta, that's a splendid idea!"

Greta smiled with relief.

Adelaide thought about it further, then said, "But we can't go knocking on doors in our pyjamas!"

"I'm sure she's seen women in housecoats before."

She considered that, then asked, "Do you think she's home?"

"It's Saturday morning ..."

"Well, I'm sure she'd love to go shopping," Adelaide decided. "She probably hasn't even been downtown yet, poor dear." She was delighted with the idea of playing tour guide on shopping day.

They quickly cleared the table of the plates, knives, and jams, took the teabag out of the pot, and covered it with a cozy. Adelaide tied her baby blue brushed nylon robe around her a little tighter. She was wearing fancy slippers with puffs of white furry stuff on the toes. She joined Greta at the hall mirror.

"Do we look all right?" she worried, patting her hair and making sure she had no jam at the corners of her mouth.

"I think so," Greta answered nervously. She wore a burgundy coloured terry cloth robe over her nightgown, and it made her gray hair look quite handsome. Suddenly she remembered her feet, and went into her bedroom to change from her worn slippers with the holes where her bunions were into a pair of Happy Hoppers.

"Does one of us have her glasses?" she asked Adelaide, coming back into the hallway.

Adelaide checked the pocket of her robe. "I have kleenex," she stated.

"I'll take mine," Greta offered and went back into her bedroom. She returned patting the case in her pocket. "All set?"

"All set," Adelaide responded. Greta opened the door, but on her way out she stopped suddenly. Adelaide bumped into her.

"Do you have the key?" Greta turned to whisper in the hush of the hallway.

"Oh— No! Good thinking, Greta!" Adelaide went back to the hall mirror. There was a door key lying on the little telephone table under the mirror. She put it into her pocket.

"Okay, got it," she returned to the door. Greta smiled grimly, and they entered the hall then, making sure their door was locked behind them.

It was a long hallway, with four or five apartments on each side. But it was well lit and the carpet was even.

"Should we ask her on our way down or on the way back?" Adelaide almost pranced in her excitement.

"Well, if we do it on our way back, we'll have the paper, so if she says no, it won't look like we came by just to ask her," Greta said.

"That way too, she might feel freer to say no if she really doesn't want to come with us."

Adelaide considered this for a minute or two. "Where did you learn to think like that?" she finally asked.

So they went down to the lobby first, at the end of the hall. Greta's back was loosening up, and she tried not to dodder. They were lucky enough to have an apartment on the first floor. The laundry room however was in the basement. They approached the rows of boxes on the wall, while Greta fiddled in her robe to get out her glasses. She took them out of the case and put them on. She leaned close to the bottom right corner, carefully reading the names on the small typed labels. She found theirs, McCall and Luxley, and pulled out the rolled-up paper. She counted and knew again that their box was two rows up and three rows over, but every time she forgot her glasses, she also forgot if it was two over and three up or three over and two up. And Mr. Chase (three over and two up) was an angry young man in a wheelchair—a motorcycle accident, someone said—and when once they took his paper by mistake, he ranted and raved and hit the boxes with the fist so loudly the whole building heard him.

"Are you sure that's ours?" Adelaide asked.

Greta peered at the name labels again, for good measure. "Yes," she said, slowly straightening. "Let's go."

They walked back through the lobby and down the hall. They stopped at #105.

Suddenly Greta was shy. "You knock, Adelaide," she said. "You're much better at this than I am."

So Adelaide stepped forward and knocked on the door.

A youngish woman, who looked like she should be a trail guide as well as the women's center researcher that she was, answered the door. She had short brown hair, and was wearing a paint-spattered sweatshirt, jeans, and track shoes.

"Hello," Adelaide began, "my name is Adelaide and this is Greta." Greta smiled as she nodded a 'Hello'. "We live just two doors down from you. And, well, we'd like to know if you'd like to go shopping with us today." There, nicely put.

"Go shopping?" the woman asked doubtfully. This is awful, she thought. My mother and sister have come in disguise to haunt me.

"Well, yes. Today is Saturday," Adelaide said, as if that explained it.

Greta came to the rescue, "Adelaide and I always go shopping on Saturday and we just wondered if you'd like to come with us. Consider it sort of a 'Welcome Wagon' gesture. You're new here and maybe you don't know anyone or don't know downtown and we just thought— Well, we thought we'd ask you." She began to feel ridiculous.

"But I don't need to buy anything," the woman answered simply. She looked at the two old ladies in their dusters or bathrobes or whatever you called those things—you could get them at every department store, she knew that—and their cute little slippers. This is priceless, she thought.

"Well," Adelaide faltered, "neither do we." She looked at the woman. She sure was a strange one.

"Then why— What are you going to buy at the stores?"

"Well, we don't really know until we go," Adelaide was getting confused. 'Going shopping' had always been a legitimate activity, something every woman intrinsically understood, like 'doing the wash' or even 'watching tv'. Now suddenly it was suspect, bereft of substance.

"There must be *something* on your shopping list—" Greta tried.

"My what?"

It was like two cultures clashing. An awkward moment passed. Then suddenly the young woman accepted their invitation.

"I'm sorry," she extended her hand. "My name is Sue. And I'd love to come. I guess I could pick up a few things."

Puzzled by her change of heart, but also pleased by it, Adelaide and Greta shook her hand. "All right then, we're just going back to look at who's got sales on today," Adelaide said and Greta held up the newspaper, "and to change." She looked at her robe with a smile of embarrassment.

"Perhaps we'll meet you back here in an hour?" Greta suggested.

"That'll be fine," Sue said, and closed her door as they left.

Adelaide and Greta didn't say a word until they were back in their apartment.

"Isn't she an odd one?" Adelaide laughed.

"Look who's calling the kettle black!" Greta laughed too.

"Hm," Adelaide agreed.

They spread the newspaper on the kitchen table and poured their second cups of tea. Adelaide turned to the section with the sales advertisements.

"Oh look at the Woolworth's ad. Is stationery on our list?"

Greta checked the little pad she'd gotten from the telephone table drawer. "Yes it is, why?"

"Well, look—typing paper, envelopes, and that white-out stuff is two for one. And spring scarves, oh and lots of kitchen things—"

"Okay, I've got Woolworth's written down. Where else?"

"Let me see … Sam's. They're a record store. And Zacks. Oh— even their sale prices are high. But put them down, they have gloves on."

Adelaide turned the page. "The I.D.A. … lots there … shampoo, soap, toilet paper— But Kresge's has those things on sale too. Let me see … 88¢ and 89¢, three for .99 and four for $1.39 … Kresge's, I think, will be cheaper."

"Okay. Where else?" Greta tried to look upside down as Adelaide turned the pages. "Anyone have sweaters on?"

"Goudies! They have all their cottons on sale and some polyester prints too!" She scanned the page. "Their whole notions department is featured! And a few things in other departments too, it looks like." They continued to go through the sales section, page by page.

"Oh goodness, it's a quarter to!" Greta had looked at her watch. "We'd better get dressed!" She finished her cup of tea, then rose from the table.

"Yes," Adelaide agreed, and shuffled the paper back together.

It didn't take them long to get ready. They each had two sets of 'shopping clothes' and it was just a matter of putting on the outfit they didn't wear the Saturday before. Low-heeled shoes were important. And their big purses, with all sorts of emergency things—you never knew what would happen on a day's trek downtown. And of course their shopping bags. Adelaide had two of the large blue and white paper shopping bags you could buy for a dime out of the boxes at Goudies. Greta liked the brightly coloured string bags that could accommodate all sorts of packages and never rip, never need reorganizing. In a few minutes, they were standing by their door, ready.

"Glasses?"

"Yes. Kleenex?"

"Yes. Shopping bags, shopping list?"

"Yes. Yes."

"Bus fare!" They opened their purses. Each had a special little change purse into which they always put the correct change for two trips before they left. Better that than to rummage while standing unsteadily on a bus, people lined up behind you.

"Do you have a nickel? I'm short—only dimes, quarters, and pennies in my wallet this week."

"Here you go."

"Thank you!"

They snapped their wallets shut then, and closed their purses.

"Okay. All set?"

"All set."

"Shall we go?"

When they knocked on Sue's door, she answered immediately. She looked exactly as she had before, with the exception of a small green knapsack on her back.

"Ready!" she said cheerily and stepped into the hall to join Adelaide and Greta.

They didn't say much on the ride down. The bus came almost as soon as they got to the stop, which was just one block away from their apartment. And it was crowded. Greta and Adelaide had to sit apart, and Sue had to stand, shuffling forward and backward as people got on and off.

After about ten minutes, Adelaide reached up to ring the bell as soon as they pulled away from the stop just before Kresge's. They always got off at Kresge's, then walked down the one side and back up the other. They caught the bus home in front of Kresge's too.

She excused herself, stood up, then began the agonizing, always anxious, process of working her way to the exit door by the time it got to the stop. She tried to see Greta, but it was too crowded. She hoped she wouldn't fall. They had told Sue ahead of time that they got off at Kresge's, but she might not be able to see when they got there—or she might see it too late. Two more seats to go. She stood by the exit door, hanging on tightly to the pole, as the bus lumbered on, peering about. Then with relief she saw Greta approaching from the rear, Sue behind her. The bus stopped, they stepped off, and gathered themselves in front of Kresge's.

"Well, Sue, welcome to downtown Kitchener," Adelaide said expansively, gesturing at the length of King Street ahead of them. She beamed. Shopping always filled her with an exhilaration she couldn't contain.

Sue did indeed look down the street. She resisted the impulse to also look down at her watch. "Shall we begin?" she said, aiming for cheer.

Adelaide's eyes glittered at Greta as she led the way into Kresge's.

She headed for the 'health and beauty aids'. There they were, soap bars in a package, three for .99. She put three bundles into the shopping basket she'd picked up at the front door. It was a square thing made of red patterned vinyl, and it always reminded her of a picnic basket. And then shampoo, 900 ml for 88¢. She looked at the selection: herbal, wheat germ oil and honey, balsam and protein, egg and lemon, aloe vera, and beer. Beer?

She turned to Sue, hoping to involve her, "Which ones do you think I should buy?"

"I don't know," Sue replied. This was not fun. The store was crowded. She did not now nor ever would care about what kind of shampoo Adelaide used. "Take one of each," she muttered as she turned away to look at something else. The door. When she turned back, she saw that Adelaide had indeed put one of each into her shopping basket. Her mouth dropped open.

They moved on, Adelaide in the lead, Greta second, and Sue tagging along behind. Things were tossed into the basket, seemingly at random—boxes of kleenex, packages of toilet paper, a cuticle scissors, a pair of nail clippers. They couldn't possibly need all of this. She smirked at their consumer addiction. "Look," she said with cruelty, "pony tail ties are on sale, six packages for 49¢!"

"What a wonderful idea!" Adelaide said and grabbed a handful. Sue thought about fabricating a forgotten appointment.

Eventually they got out of Kresge's. They passed by the I.D.A., having gotten everything more cheaply at Kresge's, then Greta stopped Adelaide in front of a hardware store.

"Look," she said, pointing to the display sign in the window, "hammers—for only $4.99."

Adelaide looked at Greta in wonder. "Magnificent!" she exclaimed.

"What do you need a hammer for?" Sue asked. "I have one you can borrow any time."

"That's kind of you," Adelaide answered. "Thank you, dear."

They entered the store and bought two. "I'm sure there's lots of things a hammer is needed for," Greta said with satisfaction, as she paid for them at the counter.

Sue thought about taking notes—surely this day could fit into the research project. It had to fit somewhere in reality.

A clothing store was next to the hardware store. Robinsons? Sue didn't notice. She was trailing by now, so passers-by wouldn't immediately know she was with them. She came upon them trying on sweaters out of a bin near the center of the store.

"What do you think about pink?" Adelaide asked, turning around to model.

"Pink's a good choice. A bright cheerful choice," Greta answered, rummaging through the piles. "And how about this yellow one too?"

"What size is it?"

Greta checked the tag, "Medium".

"Okay—this one's a Large. Shall we take a Small too?"

"Yes, let's," Greta concurred. They turned to Sue.

"You choose the third one."

Sue found herself actually looking at the sweaters, deciding what colour to choose.

"I like this one," she held up a blue and green striped sweater.

"Oh yes," Adelaide approved, "that *is* nice."

"And they feel good and warm, don't they?" Greta bunched the sweaters in her hands.

More stores. More purchases. Shoes that didn't fit, but Greta "liked" them. A couple dresses. Some socks. An extension cord. Books. Two records—Mel Torme and Michael Jackson. Both for 99¢. With that, and the multicoloured shoelaces, Sue began to wonder. When the three pairs of baby booties went into the string bag, she was sure they were both senile.

They came to Goudies. It was an old store, a classic. Grand gold lettering on the building's front. The only store in Kitchener with revolving doors, the old kind made of heavy wood, a bit of glass, and lots of burnished brass trim. It had elevators too—with elevator attendants.

"Shall we have lunch before or after we do our shopping here?"

Sue knew it was a weekly decision.

"Oh, I could use the rest now, how about you Sue?"

"Now's fine."

They passed through the revolving doors then turned left to go downstairs to the dining room. Sue looked around in disbelief. It was straight out of the 40s or 50s. A real dining room, not a cafeteria, not a food emporium.

The hostess smiled at Adelaide and Greta—they were clearly regulars—and led them to a good table. Sue followed, noting the swivel stools at the counter, stuffed and covered with red leather. The tables and chairs were wood—good, worn, wood. The room was about three-quarters full now, with shoppers. Ladies with purses and shopping bags tucked under their table, some with coats thrown over extra chairs, many with hats still on. Probably with hat pins.

"There's Magdalena," Adelaide leaned forward to say to Sue and nodded to a sweating hefty woman standing in the kitchen behind the divider behind the counter. "Best short-order cook there ever was." She waved at Magdalena who waved a floury hand back.

A waitress came and handed each a menu.

"You're new here, aren't you?" Greta asked.

"Yes, I am," the waitress replied.

"I'm Greta, this is Adelaide, and this is Sue." She introduced them all.

Sue measured the clearance under the table.

"And what's your name?"

"Ginger," the waitress replied, a little surprised.

"What a lovely name!" Adelaide said, as she opened her menu.

"Thank you," Ginger replied. "I'll give you a few minutes to decide," she smiled and left the table.

"Their club sandwiches are very nice," Adelaide offered to Sue.

"And their toasted westerns."

"And their french toast—and waffles."

"Oh—" Adelaide just remembered, "I wonder if their butterscotch rolls are ready!" She looked at Sue and put her hand on her arm, "They have the *best* butterscotch rolls here!"

"Served with real butter, of course."

"And sometimes we time it just right and get them warm out of the oven!"

They ordered. While they waited, Greta got out their shopping list and began to stroke off items.

She peered into their bags. "Did we get the envelopes yet?"

"No. They're wherever the stationery is on sale."

Greta nodded and continued updating their list.

When their food arrived, Sue dutifully joined in the comparisons and then listened to how this week's choices measured up against last week's. After they had eaten, and finished their tea, they felt refreshed and ready to carry on. The next stop was the ladies' room. It too was classic—large, with marble and mirrors. It used to have an attendant, she wasn't surprised to be told. Then they passed through a short hall that served as a small art gallery—Robert Woods oil paintings in cinnamon, nutmeg, and tangerine tones. And then they took the elevator up one flight to the notions department.

They purchased a couple yards—not metres—of this and that, several bundles from the 'ends' box, tiny sewing kits, and an umbrella from the neighbouring department. A black and white one with zebras all over it. They thought of going to look in the other departments on the second and third floors, but it was getting late, and they had the other side of King Street to do yet.

"Next time," Adelaide promised to Sue as they walked on to the exit.

Sue didn't answer.

From Goudies, they headed straight for Woolworths. The 'end' of downtown.

Greta stopped at the candy counter at the front of the store.

"Some macaroons?" she asked Adelaide.

"You know they're not very healthy."

"If I buy vitamins too?" she bargained.

"Okay," Adelaide agreed.

They waited while Greta purchased a pound of macaroons. Then they headed to the pharmacy section. Flintstones chewables were on sale. Then to the stationery section: envelopes, typing paper, white-out, and a box of pens. Oh and don't forget the scarves on sale. They had to search a bit until they found the rack, marked down in price. They chose a silver and turquoise one, a loud paisley one, and a peach polka-dot one.

"And the kitchen gadgets—they're downstairs," Greta reminded. They headed to the back of the store to the staircase, bags bulging and wire shopping baskets bumping against each other.

"Let me put some of your stuff into my knapsack," Sue offered.

She had offered earlier to carry a bag, but they refused, rightly pointing out that it was easier to carry two than one.

"That's right, you haven't bought a thing," Greta noticed.

"Oh, but you must!" Adelaide encouraged.

They picked out some wooden spoons, bowls, and melmac mugs.

Sue picked up a can opener.

"That's a good one," Greta complimented.

They accidentally wandered from kitchen to hardware, so they added a few screwdrivers and some fuses to one of their baskets. They climbed the stairs and checked out at the front of the store.

"Oh my goodness," Adelaide surveyed their bags once outside. "Look at all we have already!"

"Well remember though, this side doesn't have quite as many good stores."

"That's true."

They walked past a cigar store, another record store, and Somers' men's wear. Then the Walper Hotel. Or maybe it was the other way around. Sue wasn't paying much attention. They stopped in front of Zacks.

"Let's leave the gloves," Greta suggested with some fatigue.

"All right," Adelaide agreed. "Oh look," she noticed the store next to it, "Here's that Baskin-Rubens!"

"Baskin-Robbins," Greta corrected.

"And it's open!"

"Good," Greta said, "I could use another sit down before we head home."

"Why don't you two go on ahead," Sue said. "I'll zip into Zacks and get a pair of gloves, if you like, and I'll meet you in Baskin-Robbins."

"That's a splendid idea," Adelaide responded. "Would you dear?"

So Adelaide and Greta went ahead to Baskin-Robbins while Sue went into Zacks. She found the gloves that were on sale and picked out a pair of light green ones. She also bought two pairs of men's suspenders and a ladies' belt. Because what the hell. When she entered Baskin-Robbins, she saw that Adelaide and Greta had set their belongings at a table by the door and were up at the counter, walking ever so slowly along the ice cream freezers. Greta had her glasses on and was reading the flavours out loud.

When they got to the end, Greta nudged Adelaide. "Thirty-one flavours and they haven't got Neapolitan!" she whispered.

"Thirty-one flavours and you were going to pick Neapolitan?"

Sue saw the high school kid behind the counter laugh. Sue laughed too. Greta was right. So was Adelaide.

"I'll have the Caramel Coconut Swirl," Adelaide said then to the student.

Greta wandered along the counter again while Adelaide's cone was being prepared. Sue stepped up to order, seeing that Greta hadn't yet made up her mind.

"Chocolate and Cranberries, please."

"And I'll have the Blueberry Pecan Cheesecake—ice cream," Greta added.

They sat down, licking their cones. Greta felt tired and happy. Adelaide felt happy and tired. Sue had alternated between distaste and disbelief all day; she didn't know what she felt now.

Greta reached over with a napkin to wipe a dribble from Adelaide's chin.

"Thank you, dear. How's your Blueberry Pecan Cheesecake?"

"Very good. How's yours?"

"Excellent. I think I'll try the Strawberry Mint Sherbet next time."

"And how's yours?" they asked Sue together.

"Just fine, thanks."

When they had finished, they gathered up their parcels and purses and left the store.

"What's left?" Greta asked, trying to ignore the pain that had returned to her legs as soon as she had stood up.

"Want to cross and catch the bus here instead?" Adelaide suggested.

"Well ..."

"Yes, let's," she decided.

So they crossed, waited for a few minutes at the bus stop, almost got on the wrong one—"Greta, no, that's the Westmount—" and waited a few more minutes for the right one. It wasn't quite four o'clock so all three of them got seats. They sat through the trip in silence, rang the bell for their stop, got off the bus, then walked the block to their apartment.

Sue reached in her pocket for her keys, and let them all in.

At her door she turned to them, "Well, thanks for asking me along—"

"Oh no, we're not through yet!" Adelaide was horrified.

Sue groaned.

"You must come back to our apartment! We'll have tea and sort through what we've bought!"

Sue hesitated. She couldn't stand much more, really, but this was clearly very important to them. She could see it on their faces.

"Well, all right, but just for a bit."

Once inside, they walked first into their living room and set the bags on the floor by the couch.

"You sit, Greta, I'll put the tea on," Adelaide offered.

Gratefully, Greta sat down. After a sigh of sheer relief, she started to unpack everything. Sue helped her put their purchases onto the couch beside her. Adelaide plugged the kettle in and prepared the tea service with a plate of shortbread cookies. She went to the telephone table and brought out some sort of list, several pages hand-written and stapled together. She got her glasses from her bedroom, then joined Greta and Sue in the living room.

"Oh," she sank into an upholstered chair, "this does feel good." She looked about at all their purchases. "My, my, just look at what we have!"

"Yes, it's a lot, isn't it!" Greta agreed.

So did Sue. She had added her can opener, and the gloves, belt, and suspenders to the pile. It had seemed the thing to do. Then she resigned herself to a chair in the corner, to the edge of a chair in the corner. Adelaide got up and was back in a minute with the tea service on a large, beautiful silver tray. She set the tray on an ivory doily in the middle of the coffee table.

"Shall we begin?"

Greta nodded.

Adelaide put on her glasses and scanned the list. "The transition house didn't get their operating grant this year, the stationery stuff—the envelopes, white-out, paper, and pens—those things were for them?"

"That's right." Greta moved those items from the couch to the floor.

"We forgot stamps and a typewriter ribbon—"

"Let's put it on next week's list," Greta reached into her purse for the little pad of paper that had this week's list on it. She tore off the page and wrote down the items, starting a new list.

"All right, the hammers—they weren't on our list, were they? Who shall we give them to?"

"How about that fellow in Nicaragua—remember?"

"Perfect! And the screwdrivers too." Greta set the hammers and screwdrivers onto the floor.

"And the baby booties are for Selema, of course," she added them to the pile on the floor.

"Selema just had a baby," Adelaide explained to Sue.

"She's on our Third World list," Greta elaborated.

"The shoelaces—for Nikki?" Adelaide asked.

"She's our foster child in Peru," Greta explained this time. "And the macaroons and the vitamins."

"You spoil that child!" Adelaide reprimanded. Then she added, with mischief in her eyes, "And the pony tail ties, of course, for her lovely long black hair." Greta moved the named items to the floor as Adelaide made notes and checks on her list. Then Adelaide pointed to the candy and the vitamins, "Let's tell her she must share them with all of her classmates."

"Agreed. The umbrella?"

"The mission," Sue suggested, to her surprise. "Most of those who show up for a bed don't have an umbrella. When you live and sleep on the street, you need something to keep dry ..." her voice trailed off, as Greta put the umbrella onto the floor without question.

"Those suspenders!" Adelaide just noticed them. "They'd be perfect for Mr. Worton! You remember that gentleman in the home, Greta? Did you buy them?" she asked Sue. Sue nodded.

"They're perfect! His pants are always so loose and baggy, he's losing so much weight now, and no one has bought him new trousers— Greta ..." Greta was already adding trousers to next week's list.

"He can have the brown ones. And the red ones?"

"There's a guy I know," Sue offered, "he's also losing a lot of weight —AIDS—he was always a spiffy dresser—before ..."

"A dandy, eh? That's perfect then, they're for him," Greta put both pairs onto the floor.

The book went to a CUSO school they knew about. One of the boxes of kleenex went to a woman whose husband was a journalist; he'd been imprisoned and subjected to torture for a year now, they knew about it from Amnesty International.

"It means we cry with her," Adelaide said.

The other boxes, the soap, the toilet paper, and all the multi-flavoured shampoo went to various families in various countries from their Third World list.

Greta pointed to the clothes and kitchen things. "What about that earthquake we sent stuff to last week—do they have enough now?"

"It was a hurricane," Adelaide checked her list, "and I suppose they can always use more."

"We should've gotten another blanket …" Greta added it to their list for next week.

They looked at what was left.

"I'm going to take that paisley scarf to that woman upstairs. The one with those screaming kids?" Greta clicked her tongue, "I don't know how she does it!"

"That extension cord— Didn't we just read about some electricity generating project—Was that an Oxfam thing? Interpares?"

"Interpares, I think," Greta set it on the floor. "Good idea. The fuses too."

Sue looked at what was left. "Michael Jackson. Children's ward at the hospital?" she asked.

"Sounds good to me," Adelaide wrote it on her list.

"Agreed," Greta set it onto the floor.

"Mel Tormé, a belt, a pair of gloves, and two scarves," Adelaide took inventory aloud. "Oh, and the fabric and sewing notions."

"Let's tuck them away for now. We'll know soon who to give them to."

"Okay. Done!" Adelaide put down her list and poured the tea.

"Tomorrow we can wrap them, and then on Monday the post office will be open," Greta passed a cup of tea from Adelaide to Sue. "Have some cookies, too."

"Yes, go ahead, dear."

Sue was just sitting there, silent, stunned. She looked at Adelaide and Greta, at these two crazy ladies, these two magnificent women.

She smiled then and accepted their offering. "Thank you," she said to both of them. Then lifted her cup in a sort of toast. "To next Saturday?"

Tour of Duty

The half-filled bus arrived at the second station at eight o'clock sharp. The driver pulled up to the waiting group of fifteen or twenty people, opened the door, took a clipboard from the storage space behind the seat, and got out.

"Good morning!" It was a resonant voice, and the tone was cheerful and efficient.

"Good morning," a few answered, shuffling in the end-of-October chill. They were a mixed crowd—some with suitcases, others with knapsacks, standing with parents or partners, or in clumps of three or four, with old friends or with people just met; some faces were eager and smiling, others neutral and accepting, a few resistant.

The driver unlocked the storage compartments of the bus. Then he began to call out the names on his list.

"Arlie Boehm." A large person with light skin and lots of red hair stepped forward, put a worn knapsack into one of the compartments, and boarded the bus. There were about twenty people already inside, scattered from front to back. Arlie chose one of the few remaining window seats. They were headed to a base camp near Kenora, which was a good four hours away through country she'd only heard of. She wanted to see it.

"Susan Smith." A blond person came forward and put two suitcases into the same compartment.

"They're both yours?" the driver asked.

"Yes," she replied, a little defiant, a little afraid.

He made a note on his clipboard and called out the next name. Arlie watched as one by one, the people loaded their bags and said their goodbyes to whoever had come to see them off. Her parents were both at home, one in Listowel, the other in Hull. She had visited each one during the summer—their annual connection—and they had said their goodbyes then. Someone, thin and dark-skinned, was being hugged profusely by his mother. The young man was not embarrassed. His father reached out to shake hands, but the son embraced him too. He boarded the bus and Arlie saw him look around shyly, briefly, then smile at her as he headed to share her seat. He fit easily in to the remaining third of it.

"Hi," he said. "I'm Shahran."

"Arlie. Hi."

"You from around here?"

"Sort of. I'm going to the university here, but originally I'm from Quebec. You?"

"Yeah. I live here. Those are my parents." He pointed out the window to the couple waving proudly at their son. "I just finished high school. Thought I'd do my tour now, take the time to think about what I want to do next. What year are you in?"

"I just finished my second, of four. Decided I could use the break," she smiled thinly. "Besides, I thought that if I waited until I was done and then did the tour before I got a job, I'd forget everything. I mean, I think I'll need to apply what I've learned right away—you know, use it so I don't lose it."

"You could always work for a few years and *then* do it—"

"True, but I don't know how I'd feel about 'interrupting my career', as they say."

"Yeah, but your position would be held for you, wouldn't it? Even so," he added, "I guess it might still be a pain. I guess losing a year of seniority is a big thing for some people."

"Maybe, but everyone loses the same year—"

"But not at the same time."

"That's true." She realized only then the potential for strategizing for promotions based on seniority. Some of the people boarding the bus could well be in that position.

"And you'd still get paid, wouldn't you?" he asked.

"Oh yes, which is why a lot of employers frown on it. They used to ask on their applications if you had done your tour of duty yet, now it's illegal to ask. But," she circled back, "if I like my job as much as I expect to—intend to—hope to," she smiled at her revisions, "I think I might resent the year off, and that's another concern. I don't want to go into my tour with a feeling of resentment, y'know?"

"Yeah, I do. I think it's a *good* thing—to do what we're doing." He looked out the window and waved to his parents still standing there, stamping their feet in the cold. Then, grinning, he waved at some other people too, people he didn't know. "What are you taking? I mean, at university?"

"Veterinary science. What about you. What do you want to take?"

"Well, see, that's it. I'm not sure. I'm not even sure I want to go to university, or college. No subject I took in high school really interested me. I mean, they were all okay, it's just, nothing really— I didn't feel a *passion* for anything." He paused then. "And I want to. I want to feel passionate about whatever it is I do—" Arlie was about to second his statement, but their attention was caught by a voice behind them.

"It's a violation of my personal freedom!" It was a loud voice, and an angry one. "Pretty soon they'll be telling me what I can and cannot eat too!" Arlie recognized the voice as that of the woman with two suitcases. Susan.

"Yeah, well," the guy sitting beside her agreed, "but look at it this way. If it weren't for this whole tour of duty shit, this country's environment tax would be a lot higher. And the government would sure as hell pass it onto you know who. They'd increase our income tax, our property tax," he counted them off on his fingers, "or the garbage tax—"

"Or the sales tax and the service tax—"

"You got it. Or," he thought, "they'd increase the fines."

"Travel fines, dumping fines—" She was enjoying the litany of their victimization.

"You know," Arlie could feel the guy smile and move closer to Susan, confiding, "I'm surprised they don't fine the athletes for using more oxygen than is necessary." Susan laughed out loud then. Arlie and Shahran looked at each other with the discomfort of cowardice.

"What I can't figure out though," the guy went on, his voice a little louder, "is why us poor working sods have to do this. You'd think there'd be enough bleeding hearts and fanatics to volunteer for this kind of thing. Add to them the guys on welfare, the guys collecting unemployment, the guys in prison— I mean it's about time *they* contribute something to the economy."

"Hey Jack—"

Arlie turned to the new voice. It belonged to the person sitting across from Susan and the loud-mouth. Big and solid, with one of those beautiful black bodies and short nappy hair, he looked like an all-American football hero, ten years later.

"Name's Alec," he corrected, but didn't extend his hand.

"This tour is not about the economy, Jack." Everyone on the bus was listening to their conversation now.

"Oh no?" The tone said 'Boy, are you naive!' "What do *you* think it's about?"

The driver boarded the bus just then, closed the door, and started the engine.

"I guess we'll all find out—soon," Shahran spoke up.

"We will indeed." With a touch of embarrassment, he nodded a thank you to Shahran. "We will indeed."

There was a silence then as the bus began its journey.

At around twelve-thirty, they pulled into the base camp. The trip had been magnificent, Arlie thought. Every now and then she saw acres of deciduous forest, with splashes of gold, orange, scarlet, crimson. Gradually, the forests became completely coniferous, and evergreens stood silent among the bare spindles, some quite tall and thick. And the sky, an egg-shell blue the whole way. And lakes, dark full of sparkles.

They were instructed to take their bags with them to the food building, where lunch was waiting. Arlie and Shahran got off the bus into the cold air, waited for their stuff to be unloaded, then followed the others with zippered coats and hands in pockets, into the designated building. There were tables for six throughout the eating area, a help-yourself buffet in the middle.

In a few moments, Arlie and Shahran had served and seated themselves. Sharing their table was the football hero, an older couple, and one other person. After several preliminary comments about the food—which was *very* good—they took turns telling a bit about themselves.

"Name's Judd. I'm a cop. Fifteen years on the force." He looked at Shahran then. "That's why I should've handled that situation on the bus better."

Shahran dismissed the comment with his fork, "Don't worry about it."

"I'm Kathleen," the woman had white hair, blue eyes, and a smile full of delight. "And this is my husband, Joe."

"I thought retired people were exempt." Arlie saw they were clearly in their sixties, perhaps seventies.

"They are. But they're not ineligible. Some people move to Australia when they retire, and some go on a North Seas cruise … We decided to go on our tour of duty. Besides," she added, "Joe didn't practise last week, and he figured this was as good a way as any to avoid his piano lesson."

After a bit of laughter, Judd asked, seriously, "You take piano lessons?"

"Actually, yes, I do. Started two years ago. I've always wanted to learn how to play and, well, better late than never." He smiled, then finished the last of his bean salad.

"And it's very good for the arthritis in his hands."

"That's amazing," Arlie spoke up. "I mean, admirable. Most people stop learning when they finish school."

"I know a lot of teachers who'd disagree," Shahran said. "They'll tell you we stop learning when we *start* school." They laughed again.

"Anyone for coffee or tea? I'm heading that way," Judd got up.

"Again?" Arlie teased him. He had gone for several seconds.

"Yes, please," Shahran said, "I'll have a cup of tea."

"No problem, anyone else?" They shook their heads.

"And who are you?" Kathleen smiled at the last of their table, a very young person sitting beside her.

"Jel," she said, nervously. "It's short for Jelico." The attempt to be conversational was difficult for her. She didn't look at all sixteen, Arlie wondered if a lot of kids, runaways, lied about their age to get in. She had to admit it was a lot better than living on the streets. At least here, she'd get not only food and shelter, but a safe place from abuse, hopefully, and damaging drugs. She might even pick up a little self-esteem and confidence while she was here.

"How did you like the trip out?" Wow, Shahran was good, Arlie thought, as he skipped right over her awkwardness. And with a no-fail question that deflected attention away from any personal details.

80

"It was okay." She stared at her plate, empty quite a while ago. She had not dared go back for seconds. Arlie remembered then that Shahran had said he was full part way through his meal and had offered his plate to her. She had taken it.

"May I have your attention, please." The driver was standing up at one of the tables. The acoustics of the room were so good, there was no need for a microphone. Arlie looked carefully, for the first time, at its construction. It was very interesting architecture.

"I hope you all have enjoyed your lunch. We'd like to begin a bit of initiation now. My colleague, Xian Tseng, will give an introductory talk and answer any questions you may have. After that we'll take you on a tour of the camp. You'll have the rest of the day then to get settled in your dorms and do whatever else you want. Tomorrow, your basic training begins."

Xian stood up at another of the tables. Arlie noticed the streak of fluorescent green in the hair. Nice touch, she thought.

"Thanks, Soren. That's Soren Tullip, one of our facilitators." Judd slipped into his chair, handing one of the cups he was holding to Shahran. "First of all, I'd like to welcome all of you to this year's base camp. As you know, your training here will last four months, from November to February. Then in March you'll begin your eight-month tour assignment. For those of you who wonder about the dates, let me briefly tell you some history.

"When the program was initially set up, it was on a September to August schedule to coincide with the academic year. We anticipated that eventually most of our people would be student-aged. But it quickly became apparent that September and October were prime tour months, so the training was moved to the off months of November through February.

"As you may know, there were a lot of complaints, because then you had to miss two years of school but were 'paid' for only one. But as we learned, our environment has to come first: we have to fit into *its* schedule, we can't force it to fit into ours." She paused, then continued. "As you know, the academic world has since revamped their system and the school year is now November to October. Quite a feat. Hurray for them." There was some applause. "Many companies have since followed suit, re-defining their fiscal year.

"Over the next few months, we will not only provide you with the knowledge and skills necessary to carry out your tour assignment, we hope to also educate you to a way of life, to habits and attitudes— We hope to educate you to a lifestyle you'll continue when your tour is over, a lifestyle in which you 'make and take only what you need'." She smiled. That phrase was to be oft repeated throughout their training.

"We started with our request that you bring only one piece of luggage. You are encouraged to have only two changes of clothing—you can wear only one at a time anyway. It's one small way of getting you into the habit of using only what you need. On that note, consider the amount of food you just ate. Statistics show that Canadians eat forty percent more than they need." Arlie grinned at Judd. He grinned right back.

"Next, think of your transportation here. It was by bus. No one was allowed to arrive by private car. Bus transportation is an extension of the carpool concept. It cuts down on our fuel requirements, and, therefore, on our destructive emissions—though of course with alcohol fuel instead of fossil fuel, there's a lot less of that anyway.

"Our daily schedule follows the sun: up when it's up, down when it's down. Making maximum use of the sun's heat and light reduces our need for artificial production. When you sleep till eight then stay up till eleven, you're missing three hours of light at the start of your day and having to produce an extra three or four at night to compensate." Arlie heard someone mutter 'Give me a break!' She looked around and saw Alec at the table next to theirs.

Xian continued. "There will be dorm inspections. Though I hope none of you were, dare I say, 'stupid' enough to bring illegal substances, all non-biodegradable soap, shampoo, toothpaste, etc. will be confiscated. We'll provide you with legal and safe substitutes, no questions asked at this time. The same goes for things like aerosol spray cans, hair dryers, electric razors, and the like." Shahran saw the blond woman, sitting beside Alec, fold her arms across her chest.

"We'd like to check your medications as well: herbal teas and salves will replace many of your drugs, but you'll find out more about that in the Natural Medicines class. Are there any questions at this point?"

"What about kleenex?" a woman asked.

"We'll give you two handkerchiefs instead."

"I have a question," Alec stood up. "What is the penalty for infringement of any of your rules? Do we get spanked, kicked out, or what?" He glanced at Susan and chuckled at his suggestions. Few joined him.

"Well, first of all, we don't think of them as *our* rules. If they're rules at all, they're rules of science—facts of cause and effect. Consider non-renewable resources: use X amount per person now, and in five years there will be enough left for only Y amount of people; even renewable resources have a ceiling on their rate of use. I think you see what I mean. Our penalty, as you call it, is remedial classes. We believe that selfish and destructive behaviour is largely a matter of ignorance, in tandem with habit. Compulsory second tours of duty are rare, but not unheard of. Any other questions?" She looked around and waited a moment.

"Well, then, let me turn you over to Kelty, who'll be taking you on the tour of the base camp. Everyone, this is another of our facilitators, Kelty O'Zan."

The tour began with the kitchen at the back of the food building and the garden out behind it, which was now covered with a sort of greenhouse.

The camp grew most of its own food; the menu was vegetarian—not for any ethical reasons, but because a single serving of meat needed over ten times the land needed for the same single serving of vegetables, and agricultural land, though increasing, was still rather scarce. Thus the compost heaps in the corners of the garden served not only as practical waste disposal, they also produced much needed soil.

Joe bent down and picked up a handful of earth. He rubbed it between his fingers, then watched as it fell through the air, "What kind of worms do you have here?"

"I'm not sure. Soren will know," Kelty answered.

Joe nodded, satisfied. He'd ask Soren.

A corner of the food garden was for medicinal plants; the health building was beside the food building.

Next, Kelty took the group through the building that housed the administrative offices, the classrooms, a resource centre, and a lounge. A row of pegs hung above the coffee and tea tables. "We have, of course, a 'Bring Your Own Mug' policy, but in case you forget, there are extras in the cupboard."

The dorms were rather plain—rows of beds with shelves built into the walls. At the end of each dorm was a washroom—sinks, toilet stalls, and shower stalls.

Close to the dorm buildings, there was a laundry shed (washers only—all clothes were air-dried—that is, hung out on a clothesline). And a maintenance shed was near the middle of the camp. All of the buildings were built to catch as much of the sun as possible. And in addition, in the very center of the camp, there was an exercise generator building. Shahran saw the curiosity on Jel's face as they stood inside the building, surrounded by generators.

"How do they work?" he asked Kelty. Jel turned sharply toward him to see him smiling directly at her. She smiled shyly back.

"Well, all of these," Kelty pointed to an exercise bike, a rowing machine, a cross-country skiing simulator, a running treadmill, and a weight machine, "are identical to the original equipment designed when the fitness craze started a few decades ago. But each one has a converter attached to it to transfer or 'translate' the energy that's produced. An hour of relatively vigorous exercise on any one of these will produce enough energy to heat a twenty by forty by eight room for twelve hours, or water for four five-minute showers and twenty cups of tea, or—well, whatever. It's based on an old principle. Think of windmills."

"Does it have to be *vigorous* exercise?" Kathleen asked.

"Oh no, not any more. These converters can catch and store even the smallest amount," she smiled, "and every little bit helps."

"Well, that's it," Kelty said then. "If there are no further questions, we'll head back to the lounge. Someone will be talking to you about your schedules and telling you what dorm you're in." The group headed outside.

"Interesting place, isn't it?" Arlie was walking beside Shahran.

"Yes! It is! I wonder how much one of those exercise generators costs. I wouldn't mind getting one for our house."

"Yeah, did you see they had sort of a stand where you could put a book? When I think of all the hours I sit studying, doing nothing ..."

"Let's ask her," Shahran suggested and they ran to catch up with Kelty, their breath puffing into visibility before them.

"Kelty—" She turned and waited. "We were wondering, how much does one of those exercise generators cost?"

"Oh, they're free," she smiled at them.

"What?" They were both surprised.

"Yes," they continued toward the general building, "the Ministry of the Environment and the Ministry of Natural Resources have jointly sponsored a program whereby one exercise generator is provided free of charge to every person in Canada over sixteen years of age."

"Wow, that's quite an undertaking," Shahran said as he considered the cost.

"Not really. The generators are actually pretty inexpensive because the IEF covers most of the production expenses."

"What's the IEF?"

"Well, the generator itself was designed by a group of engineers who quit their jobs at one of the biggest hydroelectric power plants in the States. They couldn't go along anymore with the company's practice of damming every river in the world, flooding good agricultural land, destroying communities—while they still decked out every December with Christmas lights. Anyway, it turned out that the idea had a lot of support from miners, because they were being forced to mine coal so inaccessible the risk was incredible, and from loggers, because more and more of them were distressed by clearcutting acres and acres of forest, knowing that replanting didn't reproduce a healthy forest, the undergrowth never developed again. And of course, people left the nuclear power industry in droves as cover-up after cover-up was revealed about 'safe levels'. Anyway, some volunteered their labour, some offered it at half the salary they were getting before, and the rest contributed money. They called the pool of resources the International Energy Fund and directed a substantial chunk toward the exercise generator industry. The result was an excellent and inexpensive product."

"Wow." Arlie was impressed. "You should tell that story to everyone."

"I will. I just gave you a preview of your Energy class," Kelty grinned.

They had come to the general building. Kelty left them and headed toward the administrative offices, and Arlie and Shahran entered the lounge. They saw Joe and Kathleen sitting in a corner with Jelico, who was, to Arlie's surprise, actually laughing at something. Kathleen noticed them standing in the doorway and waved them over. After a quick trip to the tea table—red zinger for Shahran, and peppermint for Arlie—they went to join them.

"You don't want some tea to warm you up?" Arlie asked, seeing them empty-handed.

"Judd's bringing us some. We're a little tuckered out, and I'm afraid we consented to be waited on."

"Here you are," Judd appeared just then with a tray and handed cups to Joe and Kathleen.

"Thank you, dear," Kathleen said.

"They had hot chocolate too," he smiled and handed a cup to Jelico. She took it, but put her head down and said nothing. It occurred to Arlie that Judd would be about her father's age.

"Wasn't that a fascinating tour?" Shahran said as Judd sat down.

"Yeah," he sipped at the coffee he had gotten for himself, "especially the exercise generators. Kelty gave me the address of the company. I'm going to write to them about designing a converter for tackling machines. Just think how much energy could be produced at one football practice: twenty strong male adolescents busting their guts on the field—"

"You *were* a football player!" Arlie interrupted.

He grinned at her. Of course he was. Had been.

"I'll bet having to make what we need will certainly start affecting what we take—what we think we need." The others nodded at Kathleen's comment.

"I liked the garden," Joe offered. "And I'm surely curious about all those medicinal herbs they keep talking about. Betcha they're cheaper than any of the prescription stuff I'm on."

"Though I can't say I'm looking forward to four months without a steak."

"Or even a hamburger," Joe added to Judd's declaration, smiling at Jel. She smiled back.

"No eggs either, or milk," Kathleen worried. "They must have something to replace the calcium though …"

"I do wonder what kind of worms they use for their compost. I didn't get a chance to ask Soren."

"Worms?" Jel spoke up.

"Oh yes, you need worms. Worms are great! Don't you know what worms do?"

Jel shook her head.

"They make earth!"

Jel looked doubtful.

"They do!" Joe insisted. "They eat all the garbage in your compost heap, all your apple peels and onion skins and carrot tops, and turn it into soil. They shit soil, so to speak."

Jel giggled, a little nervously.

"Could I have your attention, please." Someone was standing by the doorway waving a file folder in the air. The social buzz died down immediately.

"Thank you. I'm Yorsk. I'm going to explain the chore schedule and the class schedule. A copy of each is posted here in the lounge, so you can write it down or memorize it or whatever.

"Over the course of your four months here, you'll rotate through eight chore assignments, spending two weeks on each: washroom duty, kitchen duty, garden, garbage, infirmary, maintenance, administration duty, and the last one is open: we hope you'll find something that needs to be done and do it for two weeks.

"The class schedule is fairly straightforward. For the first two months, you'll study all the compulsory courses: reduction, reuse, recycling, household safety, workplace safety, ethics, history, geography, biology, chemistry, and so on. The last two months will be devoted to the specialized training required for your tour assignment. Those in the air force will learn how to fly a helicopter, how, when, and where to take air samples, and how to read them, you'll learn about cloud formations and seeding, wind patterns, and so on. Those in the marines will learn water navigation—canoeing and small boatcraft, as well as scuba and skin diving—how, when, and where to take and read water samples, the ins and outs of limestone dumping, plankton farms, etc., etc. And those in our land forces will learn how to drive a jeep, how to take and read soil as well as flora samples, you'll also learn about reforestration and a bunch of other stuff," he smiled. "Any questions?"

Alec raised his hand, but then thought the better of it. Like everyone else, he was tired and really just wanted to settle in and relax until the evening meal.

"Oh, and your dorm assignments are posted in that corner of the lounge," he pointed.

The room gradually emptied then as people finished cups of tea, coffee, and hot chocolate, and checked their chore and dorm assignments. Kathleen, Joe, Jel, and Arlie were assigned to one dorm, along with several other people they hadn't met yet; Shahran, Alec, and Susan were in the next dorm; and Judd was in yet another. Segregation by sex had gone out of practice as sexism had faded and homosexuality had come out of the closet. Personal privacy was still possible because toilets were in individual stalls, just like in the old segregated washrooms, as were, now, showers. Each bed also had a curtain, like those found in hospitals, that you could pull around you whenever you wanted to be alone.

"Shit!" Someone was upset with a chore assignment.

"I bet Alec got washroom duty," Shahran giggled at Arlie.

"He's probably never cleaned a toilet in his life!" she responded, as they went to wash out and replace their cups.

It was three o'clock, two hours until supper. It didn't take long to unpack one knapsack.

"I'm going to check out the resource centre. Would you guys like to come?" Arlie was sitting on her bed, looking toward Joe, Kathleen, and Jel.

"No, you go ahead dear, Joe and I are going to have a little nap."

"Jel?" The girl hadn't yet been able to meet her eyes.

"No." She didn't mean it to be rude. "I guess I'll just hang around for a bit."

"Okay, see you at dinner," Arlie left the dorm and called out as she came to the next one.

"Shahran!"

His head appeared at one of the windows. "Yeah?"

"Want to check out the resource centre?"

"Yeah! Wait a minute—" He came out the door, smiling broadly. They began to walk toward the general building.

"What are you smiling about?"

"You know that Alec character? And Susan?"

"Yeah …"

"Well, Alec's still fuming about his washroom duty. He says there's no way he's going to clean toilets and sinks. And Susan—have you noticed how there's only one waste basket in the whole dorm—a little one at the door?"

"No, actually, I hadn't."

"Well, she moved it to her bed. I think it's half full already."

"Wait till she gets garbage duty."

Shahran burst out laughing then. "She has it already—that's *her* first assignment!"

Arlie joined in his laughter.

"But you know," he said, suddenly sober, "I don't think she connects, you know what I mean?"

"Yeah." Arlie thought of a lot of people—she thought of one of her closest friends: Ramanth gave money twice a year to the Ecologic Group, and yet she used disposable diapers. And the donation wasn't to relieve guilt. She just didn't, as Shahran put it, 'connect'.

"Yeah," Arlie repeated. "I know exactly what you mean." Some essential understanding of cause and effect was missing. Was it because the effect was not direct? And/or not immediate? And/or not visible? Are we so limited, crippled, by time and vision?

And so basic training began at the Kenora Base Camp.

Once Alec realized that he didn't actually have to touch the stuff—rubber gloves and a smock were provided—he *did* clean out washrooms for two weeks. Unfortunately the fact that the non-chemical cleansers he was using did as good a job as all the other brands used by people everywhere was lost on him.

Jel's first chore duty was the garden. She was reluctant, quiet, shy about it. Actually she was truant the first day. Kathleen was quick to realize that she probably had never seen a garden before. So on the second day, Joe went with her. And every day after that. He was delighted to get two garden duties, and as far as he was concerned, accompanying Jel was 'something he saw that needed to be done'. After the first three days, Jel was sitting and talking with Joe about sprouts and shoots and seeds—and worms—like an old pro.

"There's something about it that she really likes, something that's different from what I see in it," Joe said to Kathleen one day, trying to figure it out.

"Well," Kathleen offered, "it's harmless, it won't hurt her. Ever."

Kathleen, who had infirmary duty, was often in the garden too—at the other end, learning to identify and care for various medicinal plants. "And it's simple, but not boring. And she doesn't have to talk to it. It doesn't ask her questions."

"Let's buy her a kitten," Joe said suddenly. "I mean, after our tour, let's give her a kitten. A little orange fluffy one."

"Oh Joe—" Kathleen kissed him.

Susan, on garbage duty, had the three Rs drilled into her until she was sick of reducing, reusing, and recycling. When she said so, she was switched to composting. One of her tasks during the course of the two weeks was to weigh the garbage she handled. The base camp posted the average per person per day, to compare it with the 1990 Canadian figure of 1.7 kg. The camp's record was less than half that, 0.7 kg, and it was an unspoken challenge for each group to better that figure.

One of the biggest reasons for their low per person figure, Shahran discovered on kitchen duty, was their use of bulk products. Because of that, the camp went through very little packaging. In addition, since a lot of packaging was made from recyclable newsprint, the ink treated somehow so it didn't rub off, they recycled what they did go through. Unlike most people who bought individually-wrapped products.

Arlie, on maintenance, was impressed with the fact that the crew used bicycles to get around the camp, not a fleet of pick-up trucks. They did have one pick-up, but it was used only when its strength or carrying capacity was required (most of the bicycles were fitted with small carts). And it got an amazing 100km/l.

Actually she learned that it wasn't all that amazing. The technology to create vehicles that could get 70-80km/l existed as early as 1970, but it took much longer than that for the auto industry to use it. And the extra 20 km was due to a few simple modifications Soren showed her.

Another thing that struck Arlie's attention was that the work orders, when they were on paper, were on small bits of 'beige is beautiful' unbleached paper; and, like all the handouts in class, both sides were used before tossing them into the recycle bin.

However most inter-office communication was electronic—erasing and reusing space on a computer chip was less energy-expensive than recycling and reusing a piece of paper; also, conveyance of the former was cheaper than that of the latter. And internally, chalk and blackboards or waterink pens and whiteboards were used a lot. *And*, Arlie was delighted to see, a lot of 'magic pads' were in personal use for things like 'things to do' lists—she'd had one as a kid: you wrote on it with a pressure stylus and when you lifted the plastic film separating it from the underpad, the words 'disappeared'.

She met Judd in the laundry room one day. He was doing his own clothes as well as those of several other dorm members (even though the washer had a 'tiny' load setting, it was taken for granted that people would pitch in to make the use of it worthwhile, that is, energy-efficient).

"Hey Judd, how's it going?"

"Oh, not bad. Not great though either." She raised her eyebrows in question. "I'm on administrative duty this first time, and it's not exactly my cup of tea. I hate the paperwork at the station too. But I'm learning a few interesting things."

"Like what?"

"For starters, the word 'paperwork' isn't very appropriate here, have you noticed?"

"You mean all the whiteboards and magic pads—'

"Yeah! I used to feel good when I saw our recycling bin overflowing with paper. And now—"

"'Make and take only what you need'?"

"Yeah! And the whole 'lateral organization' thing, as opposed to hierarchy—you know, having a committee instead of a boss—that's new to me. And I think I like the idea. And 'collective decision-making' instead of top down directives or even majority rule. I wouldn't want to use that on the beat, but it might be helpful at the station."

"Going to reorganize the police administrative structure?" she asked, half-joking. "Aren't cops, by and large, a rather conservative rule-fixated bunch?"

"I suppose … But hey," he grinned, "'the times they need a changin'."

His load was done, and she put hers in as soon as he'd taken his out. Then she followed him outside to help him hang it on the clothesline.

"Have you seen the pens they have around here?" he asked.

"Yeah. On dorm inspection, they took my Bic—disposable, of course—I hadn't really thought about that—and gave me one of them."

"They're great. Fine, medium, or thick, and refillable without even touching the ink. Same with their typewriter ribbons. You re-ink them by snapping them into a little contraption and cranking a handle. Totally mechanical and not at all messy."

She grabbed one end of the bedsheet while he pulled at the other. They stretched it over the line.

"And the typewriters themselves—not electric, you know, but just as fast, just as smooth—"

"Yes, I've seen them," Arlie said. "We had to repair one yesterday, I'm in maintenance," she explained. "And the ditto machines. Just like the old ones but with a non -toxic chemical."

"Yeah, no photocopiers around here. I never realized how energy-expensive they were!"

"Have you noticed the light bulbs?" she asked then. "They last forever! We never have to change them!"

"Really?"

"Yeah, apparently the technology's been around for almost a century, but we've been 'building in', 'planning' obsolescence. I was so angry when I found that out! And apparently that's the way it's been with a lot of things!"

"Yeah," Judd agreed, grimly, "like human existence on earth."

It was January 1. Half-way through base camp. They were in the food building, celebrating the new year with a feast—in variety, not in quantity. Arlie, Shahran, Joe, Kathleen, Jel, and Judd were sharing the table that had come to be theirs.

"So now that we're through with the basic education courses, what was the class you think you'll remember most?" Kathleen tossed the question out to the table.

"The oil spill" Shahran said without hesitation. "Remember the kids' swimming pool filled with saltwater, rocks, and sand and then the one measly cup of crude oil Xian dumped in?"

"Yeah. First, someone tried pouring in some kind of neutralizer," Arlie recalled.

"Which didn't work."

"Nor did my liquid detergent," Kathleen said "It cuts through grease, so I thought—"

"And remember Joe patiently scooping it off the surface with a paper cup—" Shahran smiled at him.

"Well ..."

"And Susan! Remember what Susan tried?" Judd was laughing. "She tried to vacuum it up!"

"Don't laugh," Shahran said, "her method worked the best, didn't it?"

"Better than that magnet idea. Who thought of that?"

"I wonder if that wasn't what gave Susan the vacuum idea—"

"Remember the person who suggested freezing it and then just chunking the oil layer off?"

"Brilliant idea, I thought," Joe commented. "It has a certain elegance. But you can't freeze a whole ocean."

"Well, not without serious side effects ..." They paused on that one, chewing thoughtfully.

"I remember the corporations class the most," Kathleen said.

"You mean all those company profiles?"

"Yes—who owns who, who makes what, how they make it, where they make it, the lawsuits, the recalls—"

"I'll never shop the same again," Shahran said.

"I liked the ethics course the most," Joe took his turn next. "I agree with a lot of what we're doing now, but I have to be able to justify it, you know? I have to have a basis, an answer for the question 'why'."

"It helps to talk with people like Alec too, doesn't it?" Judd offered.

"Well, yes," Joe misunderstood. "That young man raised a lot of good points that I hadn't thought about. About rights and responsibilities and priorities! I still disagree with him. But now I can tell him why." The others nodded.

"What about you, Arlie?"

"Oh, I liked all the science classes—biochemistry in particular. I'd heard of PCBs and CFCs before, and DDT and TTC—"

"And lead and mercury—"

"Dioxin, sulfur dioxide, nitrogen oxide, carbon monoxide—"

"And carbon *dioxide*—"

"And selenium and toxaphene—"

"Chlordene, phosphates—"

"Plutonium—"

"But—" Arlie held up her fork to halt the proud display of their newly acquired knowledge, "it's really interesting to see the actual molecular structure, to see in indisputable black and white what happens when this molecule meets that molecule—"

"The cause and effect—"

"Exactly. Remember what Xian said that very first day about the rules not really being rules but just facts of cause and effect? It's absolutely true!"

"Like with the ozone, and the rainforests—all that legislation, all those rules ..."

"Yes, if we had just accepted the facts of cause and effect *as* facts—*those* are the only rules we would've needed." Arlie's sadness hung for a moment over the table.

"Remember the cancer class?" Kathleen added as a footnote.

"Yeah. How many millions of dollars were poured into various cancer foundations?"

"When all along the cure for cancer was simply to stop putting carcinogens into the air we breathe and the soil we eat of."

"It's so simple it makes us look like retards, doesn't it?" Judd stated.

Then he changed the tone a bit. "I liked the history course. All those chronologies of ecological disasters and how they could've been avoided." He added, "I wish my history courses in school way back when had taken that approach when they taught us about all the wars."

"And Kim's class on 'Great Decisions'—most of which were made by people with economic power, not political power—"

"Most of which were not even recognized as decisions—"

"Most of which we're still recovering from—"

"Any votes for the geography course?" Arlie asked. "'Hot Spots'— remember the list of uninhabitable places?"

"*And* the list of places once in critical condition, now healthy—"

"What about 'Trends and Forecasts'—*that* was a great class."

"The simplicity of 'If—then'," Joe mused.

"What about you Jel, what class did you like best?" Kathleen asked.

She hesitated a moment. "I understood them all" she said, smiling and looking up at everyone. One by one, they nodded as they ate, understanding her answer in their own way.

"So," Shahran reached for the bottle of ketchup (the little packets so popular in cafeterias had been discontinued years ago), "basic education is over. Tomorrow we all start our specialized training. Everyone know what they're going to do?" He looked around the table. The tours were usually assigned according to need and skill. And most people were content to go where and do what was needed most. But sometimes one was free to choose; you could also apply for a transfer.

"I'm putting my veterinary knowledge to good use on a land tour," Arlie said. "I'll be tagging animals for part of the time, and then I'll be doing a lot of the routine tests on deer, fox, rabbits—"

"And seagulls and dolphins? Or are you going to stick to land?" Kathleen asked.

"Land, I think. I know mammals more than anything else."

"Guess you'll be doing autopsies too?"

"Yeah," she realized sadly, "I guess so."

"I'm going on a land tour too," Joe spoke up. "But while Arlie's doing the fauna, I'll be doing the flora: soil sampling, measuring and observing growth patterns ..." This didn't surprise anyone.

"Me too," Jel said softly. The others smiled. Their various notes to facilitators recommending that placement had not been overlooked. Or necessary.

"Kathleen?"

"Well, I've always wanted to learn how to fly a helicopter," her eyes danced, "but I guess I'd rather spend the year with these guys," she jerked her thumb at Joe and Jel. Jel smiled shyly. "So for the next two months I'll be specializing in Earth Studies too."

"I've been asked to go on a patrol tour," Judd spoke up. "You know, to the areas with no logging, fishing, or hunting, or to areas with restricted flying and driving. So I'd take the Ecology Laws class for my specialized training. But ..."

"But?"

"Well, I'm not sure I want to do that. I know it's a good use of my skills, but I'm tired of it. Well not tired of it," he quickly amended, "I mean I'll always be a cop, I like being a cop, but I'd also like to do something different ..."

"Well, you have the weekend to think it over," Kathleen assured him.

"Shahran? What's your tour assignment?" Joe asked.

"Well," he paused dramatically, "they've asked if I'm interested in becoming a facilitator!"

"Here?" Arlie was surprised and pleased.

"Or at another base camp somewhere."

"And?"

"I said yes! Yes!" he laughed happily. "So, I take pedagogy courses for the next two months, as well as psychology and sociology. Then my tour is served as a facilitator's apprentice."

"You don't need a degree or anything?"

"If I decide to go ahead with it, yes, I'll embark on extensive Environmental Studies training." He was clearly delighted.

"Well, congratulations!"

"Thank you!"

"Anyone know about Susan and Alec?" Arlie felt a little embarrassed asking, the two of them had been their source of humour all through basic training.

"Yes. Alec's been assigned to a research group on corporate and environmental law," Shahran informed them.

"Perfect," Judd said. "And he'll love it."

"And Susan?"

"Well, I heard Susan quit last week."

"Quit?"

"How can she quit?"

"Apparently she just walked out of the camp one day."

"With or without her two suitcases?" Arlie couldn't resist, but even she didn't laugh.

"So what happens now? She'll have to come again?" Kathleen asked.

"I guess so."

"And if she refuses?"

"Apparently there's a very high fine." They were silent for a moment, working through the justice of it, the necessity of it.

Shahran broke the silence. "A toast!" He raised his glass, and the others followed.

"To a new year, of making and taking—" he paused, waiting for them to join in.

"—only what we need'!" they chorused loudly, clinking glasses with each other to seal their pledge.

The Nine O'Clock News

"Whatcha watchin'?" Jessie came into their living room freshly showered and towelling his black hair. He had been at the garage till eight. Better than the last few nights, anyway. One of his old high school teachers—his art teacher, and the best teacher he'd ever had, in fact—had brought in her Porsche for some work, and he'd promised to do it himself. (The job would require lots of test drives, of course.) (It was a *black* Porsche.)

But Hank (her real name was Mirabelle but since that was ridiculous, her friends called her Hank) (good thing too—when Jessie came along, he almost broke off their first date when someone told him what her real name was) had just gotten home herself, her shift at the bank ending at seven-thirty this week.

"The news," she answered, moving over for him to sit beside her on the couch. She had set their dinner on their vintage Goodwill coffee table. Wieners in a sort of tomato-and-onion sauce, pork-and-beans, and mashed potatoes.

"You mean *W5* or something? The news isn't on now."

"Yes it is. This is *The Nine O'clock News.*"

"Hi," a voice from the tv said, "and welcome to *The Nine O'clock News.*" She grinned at him and put her fork on top of her head like an antenna.

He grinned back and tossed his towel at her, then sat down, shovelled a forkful of wieners into his mouth, and turned his attention to the tv. He saw three people sitting on a couch talking. Two, actually: one guy was sitting in a wheelchair.

"This is the news?"

"Yeah, why?"

"It doesn't look like it. It doesn't look … professional," he tried to clarify.

"What do you mean?"

"Well, you know, they don't look very business-like."

"What, a profit motive should be part of the news?"

"No, that's not what I meant by business—"

"Then what did you mean?" she persisted playfully.

"You know, look at what they're wearing!"

She looked. The white guy had on light-coloured pants and a sweater. The other one, the one who was reading the first item—something about solar energy cars in Los Angeles—was wearing a blue shirt, long sleeves rolled up a bit, and jeans. And the woman, a large East Indian woman—Hank liked her the best, she always said exactly what she thought—had on a multi-coloured sari.

"Yeah? So? What's your point?"

"Come on, you know what I mean, do they look like experts?"

"I don't know. How can I tell by looking at them? Should there be some mark on their forehead?" She turned back to stare at the tv with mock intensity. "Actually Charid has one," she pointed with a wienered fork. "See that red dot there, right between her eyes? Maybe that's the official 'dot of expertise'." She popped the wiener into her mouth then continued thoughtfully. "The other two don't have a dot, though I think …" she squinted at the tv, "I think George …" and pressed her face against the screen, "I think George has a pimple!" She turned back to Jessie holding her face still squeezed out of shape, "Does that count?"

"Cut it out," Jessie was laughing.

"Well! What *do* you mean?" She scampered back beside him on the couch. "Do you think you look like an expert crawling under a car with grease up to your armpits?"

"Yeah, actually, I think I look pretty sharp in my uniform." He added then, grinning, "Mrs. Morray said so when she dropped of her Porsche."

"Oh, your uniform makes you an expert does it? And when you work on your own cars here on the weekends in your jeans and that old pyjama top, then you're *not* an expert anymore and you don't know what the hell you're doing?"

George turned to face Charid. "I think you'll like our next item …"

"He's got a pony tail for god's sake!" Jessie cried out, waving his fork at the screen.

"It's called a rat's tail. And so what? You sound like the bank when they wanted to fire Zeebo because she spiked her hair and dyed it pink. She was suddenly 'unprofessional'—remember? That woman is the fastest teller in the west! And she always always *always* balances at the end of the day!" She held up three fingers on each hand and looked puzzled, as if the concept was unfamiliar to her.

"I thought you were going to sneak a penny into her till one day."

"I tried," Hank mumbled, her mouth full of beans. She swallowed then, "but she caught me! I swear she's got eyes in the back of her head! I tell you if we're ever held up by gangsters, I hope they go to her wicket. She'd be able to recognize their *fingerprints* in a line-up! Three years later! Blindfolded!"

"With their snowmobile gloves on." Jessie had met Zeebo at a staff Hallowe'en party.

"A senior citizen's nursing home in Nova Scotia," George was reading, "Harpin's Manor, accepts residents' pets. In fact, residents without pets are encouraged to get one if they like. A few students from a nearby senior public school have been given part-time jobs to come at eight-thirty, noon, and after school to help look after the animals."

"The students take the animals for walks?" Charid asked.

"Well, apparently the property is fenced in—"

"For some of the happier wanderers?" Arnie interjected the question, with a smile.

"You got it. So the animals are free to roam and, therefore, already get a fair amount of exercise. But some of the residents need help feeding their pets: one woman can't bend low enough to set the dish on the floor, and her dog is too old now to jump up on her bed to get to it. And then there's litter boxes and bird cages that need to be cleaned."

"Any hamsters and guinea pigs?" Charid asked.

"Yes," George scanned the report he was holding, "and also those long floppy-eared rabbits. Apparently, they have become quite popular."

"Well, it's about time, isn't it?" Charid responded to the news. "I mean studies have shown for years the positive benefits of having a pet: something to talk to, something to hold—and something that needs you."

As George set the report onto the coffee table in front of them, Arnie added to her comments, "And of course for those with pets before—"

"Yes! I can't imagine being seventy or eighty and having to say good-bye to my dog of maybe ten years! I'd rather die! Really!" Charid was nodding her head for reinforcement. "And take my dog with me if it came to that!"

"What would you do?" Hank asked Jessie. "What would you do if you had a dog for ten years and you were seventy-five and you had to move into a home cuz you kept forgetting to turn off the stove or something?"

Jessie was remembering Bernard, his St. Bernard, whom he'd had to leave for two years when he went away to college. "I don't know," he answered. "Sell the stove."

"And in the House," Arnie was speaking, "the following Bills are being discussed. Bill 304 is an amendment to the CMP, Canada's Medical Plan, to include cosmetic surgery for birth defects on the list of eligible procedures. Bill 342 is an amendment to the Immigration Act allowing all those seeking safety to enter Canada, regardless of national origin and occupational potential."

"Wow, that's a biggie," George commented.

Arnie agreed then continued, "Also under discussion are motions to increase the garbage tax, to expand rail service in the North, and ..."

"This is weird," Jessie observed.

"What?"

"Well, you don't usually hear this kind of stuff on the news," he waved his knife at the tv.

"Yeah. Neat, isn't it?" Hank went out to the kitchen to get more milk. "They have a rule," she called out, continuing, "no more than ten percent of the items can feature death or physical injury, and more time has to be given to conflict resolution not involving violence than to that that does."

"That must cut out quite a bit." Jessie was distracted for a moment then by the tail end of a joke Arnie was telling, about how many Canadians were needed to build a railroad. "So what do they report on?"

"What do they report on?" she echoed as she returned. "There's *lots* of news that doesn't involve violence. It just started this week, but so far they've covered all sorts of talks: arms talks of course, rather than the use of, labour negotiations, rather than the riots—"

"Did they ever give a reason? I mean, for their restriction on content?" Jessie interrupted.

"Yeah. Partly it's a value judgement. They think conflicts worked through without violence are more important, more *worthy* of our attention. Partly it's a conditioning thing—" Jessie raised his eyebrows, so Hank went into an explanation. "They figure we make violence special, we make it sensational, by watching it. By paying attention to it, we're saying it's worth attention. You know, like when there's a fight, like at school, and everyone goes to watch. If everyone was bored with it—and frankly I am, now—and just walked away, or didn't go in the first place, do you think the guys would keep fighting?"

"Maybe. Depends what they were fighting about."

She made a face at him as if to say 'Oh come on!'

"Okay, you're right," he conceded, then qualified, "they wouldn't fight as much. Having an audience makes it harder to stop, to give in, to give up. So *not* having an audience … yeah."

"And partly—" Hank began to continue but then stopped.

"You know," George was saying, "in other countries, people have been paying by the pound for their garbage disposal for years."

"And has it cut down on the amount of trash?" Charid asked.

"Yes! Everyone in Europe has a compost heap, and in Sweden it's *illegal* to throw out anything that can be recycled!"

"So do you think an increase in the garbage tax is the way to go?"

"Well if …"

"And partly," Hank resumed, "it's a manipulative thing. Their rules about content."

"They said that?"

"Yeah. They said that if they were going to manipulate us, the least they could do was be upfront about it. They think that the more people hear about good things, the better they'll feel, and the more they'll try to *do* good things, see—listen—" she broke off quickly.

"Don't forget," George was saying, "if you have an opinion on any of these issues or an idea you think should be mentioned and considered, call your MP."

"If you don't know who your MP is," Charid added, "or what their phone number is, call 1-800-471-1111 and just say where you live." The number appeared on the screen under the title 'MP Directory'.

"See? When *they* say their news is 'action-oriented'," Hank said, "they mean that it's news we can take action about, not that it looks like a Stallone movie."

"*And,*" Arnie stuck his head into camera view, "if you don't *know* where you live—"

Charid pulled him back laughing.

"And without all the Stallone stuff, they can fill an hour?" Jessie asked then, chuckling at Arnie.

"Easily! Do you know how many survival think tanks there are? People all over the *world* are getting together to work out strategies to save us. 'Physicians for the Prevention of Nuclear War', 'Secretaries for Tomorrow'—"

"*I've* never heard of either of those groups before."

"Exactly!" Hank said. "They also cover things like medical breakthroughs. And they have an 'ordinary hero' spot: every night they highlight some ordinary person doing something pretty fantastic or just something good—"

"The company plans to begin expansion in March," Charid was saying, "creating 40,000 new jobs. However, environmental groups agree that the ground water of the entire area will be at risk. One of the chemicals used in the wood treatment process is arsenic, and if the new facility is constructed according to plan, run-off will leach from the stored wood into the soil." Charid went on to explain exactly what the problem was, what the company had said to the protesting groups, and what the Ministry of Environment was doing about it.

"They seem to spend a fair amount of time on each item," Jessie noted.

"Yeah. Most news programs have a length restriction of thirty seconds per item. They don't follow that rule."

"The company's president is Robert Dusseldorf, their address is 1426 Broadway Street, Timmins, Ontario, and their products are marketed under the name TimmberWood." She threw the item onto the table in disgust.

"See? So we can write a letter or boycott the company."

"Do something negative," he chided her.

"Well, negative for the company, but positive for the groundwater, the whole ecology there. You can write about the positive things too, tell companies when you support what they're doing. Didn't they give the address of that old age home? I know for sure they give dates and places of meetings and rallies and work parties—"

"Work parties?"

"Yeah. Like instead of just saying 'A tornado hit so and so,' they'll say 'Rescue squads are meeting at 6:00 a.m. at the community centre,' for instance."

"Or 'Money and canned goods can be sent to so and so'," Jessie was beginning to understand the idea. "I wonder if the newspapers will start to do the same thing."

They watched a bit more, finishing the food on their plates.

"I wonder how they decided on two men and one woman."

"No," Hank replied, "actually, there's six of them."

Jessie held up two fingers on one hand and one on the other, looking puzzled. She laughed.

"None of them needed a full-time newscaster's income, so they all job-share. George shares with a woman named Pat O'Malley—she's neat—she's in her sixties—they alternate every day. And Arnie shares with James Cree—"

"Is he?"

"Is he what?"

"Cree?"

"Oh," she thought about it, for the first time. "I guess he might be. They're on a 'four days on, four days off' shift change, I think, I've only seen him once. And Charid shares with someone named Anna Krstanovich. I haven't seen her at all yet, I don't know how they rotate." Hank stopped, her attention caught again by an item.

"CLAND, Canadian Lawyers Against Nuclear Destruction, is taking the federal government to court. They're charging the government with conspiracy to commit murder because of the nuclear weapons it continues to produce," Arnie was reading from the small sheaf of papers he was holding. "If the case is successful, it will be declared unconstitutional for the government of Canada to produce any nuclear arms, in part or in whole, directly through manufacture or indirectly through foreign contracting."

"That's an interesting idea," Jessie commented, "I wonder if it'll work."

"I guess we'll see. They'll probably present updates."

"Back to what you said about their job-sharing," Jessie said, "how can they afford it? Not to work full-time?"

"I don't know," Hank replied. "They must each have another source of income. They all said they'd rather have extra time than extra money. Arnie has new baby twins and likes spending entire days with them rather than just evenings. And—"

"How do you know all this?" Jessie was on his way to the kitchen with his dishes.

"Oh, they talked about themselves a bit on the first show."

He stopped then and addressed the living room of their apartment. "Hi. My name is Arnie. And I'm an—"

"What's wrong with that?"

"It's so ... unprofessional!"

"What's unprofessional about it?"

"A professional's not supposed to get personally involved. You're supposed to be objective, impartial."

"There's no such thing. Unless you're a robot. They also talked about that. These guys *react* to the news they tell. They're human! And, usually, conscious! They're not like most of the clowns who say only what someone else tells them to say, in a practised voice that covers three octaves in order to sound interesting. These people don't have to *sound* interesting, they *are* interesting! If Charid thinks an item is a crock of shit, she says so. And George—"

"But that's all wrong!" he came back. "They're manipulating you, telling you how to react!"

"They are not! Just because Charid thinks something is bullshit, that doesn't mean I'm going to think so too. Nor George nor Arnie. They're always tossing things back and forth—"

"You don't think the government should *ever* be above—or outside—the law?"

George was asking Charid.

"No!" she was vehement. "What's the point of working long and hard for laws that guarantee individual rights and freedoms if the government can toss them out whenever it pleases—declare a state of national emergency and impose martial law!"

"But what if it's for our protection?"

"As in 'for our own good'? George," she scolded gently, "we're big boys and girls now. We don't need a daddy—or a big brother—looking after us. We can—and we should—look after ourselves!"

"But—"

"You think nuclear weapons are for our protection too, don't you?" she challenged.

"See?" Hank was pleased. "Being subjective makes more sense! Dropping an item from out of nowhere into a vacuum, being 'objective' and 'impartial'—that doesn't work! No context, no meaning!"

"Well, portraying both sides is kind of like being objective."

"Both? Who said anything about two sides? Sometimes they all agree, but usually between the three of them, they come up with six or seven sides."

"'Wild Kingdom' will be back after these messages," Arnie deadpanned to the camera.

Hank burst out laughing.

"See? Just that! How can they expect to be taken seriously if they aren't even serious themselves?"

"What, when someone cracks a joke, or smiles, they blow all credibility? What kind of logic is that?"

He had no answer.

"No sports?" he asked then, noting that it was almost ten o'clock.

"Too trivial. This *is* a serious show," she smiled.

"Weather too trivial too?"

"Well, yeah, on a day to day basis. I mean millions of people live quite adequately not knowing if it's going to be eighteen degrees tomorrow or nineteen. Or what the chance of precipitation is. They do have environmental reports though: global trends, and climate changes, the condition of the ozone, pH readings—that kind of thing."

The Nine O'clock News was signing off. Hank got up to take her dishes into the kitchen.

"And it's on every night? At nine o'clock?"

"Looks like it," she paused at the doorway. "I guess someone finally figured out that not everyone works nine to five and goes to bed at eleven. Besides, it does seem silly for every station to put their news on at the same time. That way you can only watch one and you have to choose. If they staggered the times, someone who likes to watch the news can do it whenever it's convenient, and they can watch more than one program."

"Yeah, but given a choice between the news and whatever else is on at *nine* o'clock, who do you think will choose to watch the news?"

"So," Arnie was looking out at them. "This is goodnight," he grinned, "from Larry, Curley, and Moe."

"We did!" She grinned at him.

Mittsiball

Seckie raced around the gym, clearing the low hurdles as if they weren't even there, hesitated at the end of the lap, then, just because it felt so good, did it again.

Remers, at the sidelines, stared, mouth open in a smile, then said to Kern, "Doesn't Seckie look fantastic?" Kern nodded in admiration. They both hooted and whistled as their Edwin Moses passed them by.

Still waiting on the floor, at the end of the gym, was the fluorescent green tennis ball. Seckie picked it up and threw it at the target ten metres away. She missed. Figures, she laughed, as she ran to retrieve the ball and try again.

"You've got it this time," she heard Remers encourage, "No problem!"

Yeah! Zowee! Next is five—where's yellow five?

She looked up and saw Ditch halfway across the gym ready to throw. Seckie nodded then ran a few steps forward to catch the purple-and-orange striped playball.

Remers and Kern yelled "TWO!" and Seckie did a little touchdown jig. Ditch grinned then grabbed the basketball off the floor at red six.

The balance beam was five. Running to it, Seckie tucked the playball under one arm, and using the other for balance, quickly walked across the beam. She added sound effects to her dive onto the crashpad.

She looked up then to pass the ball, but Ditch was still doing lay-ups. And it was too far. Pratzsky—where the hell was Pratzsky? At the end of the gym crawling the tunnels. Pratzsky never looked for the ball anyway. Pratzsky was not a good team player. Pratzsky gets a 'D' in group work.

Six—oh yeah—six was tires. Seckie trotted to the middle of the gym. She did not like tires. Tucking the playball under her arm again, she took a moment to rehearse: one-two-one-two-one-one-two-one-two-two. Okay, here goes. She carefully hopscotched through the maze of black rubber. All right! If you had the rhythm right, it *was* easy! Remers had always said so. But then Remers could dance the polka without looking at her feet. Seven, yellow seven was—

Finally! The ball sank through the net, Kern let out a cheer, and Ditch, eager to make up for lost time, spun around looking for red seven. Aha—the bleachers—moonwalking. In three seconds flat, she'd put on the ankle weights and had begun to run up and down the stairs. The harder she ran, the funnier it'd feel when she took off the weights and watched her legs float away with every step. Up and down, up and down, that's two, up and down, she felt her heart pound, up and down, her body sweat, up and down, that's five!

Okay—next—she laughed at her legs doing *grands battements* all on their own—whee!—underwater, outerspace—

Next was eight, rope climbing. No problem. Then she was at nine, monkey bars. And ten was push-ups. Whose idea was this, her shoulders screamed.

"Come on, Ditch, four more!" Remers called out. She groaned and pushed ... up. Twice she saw Seckie look over to pass but it was impossible. What the hell was Pratzsky doing?

Pratzsky was doing blue nine: bicycling his ass off, his eyes on the speedometer. As soon as he hit 35 kmh, he scrambled off and ran to blue ten: putting. He picked up the golf club and in one try, succeeded. "Yes!" he yelled and looked up to see if anyone saw him. Seckie saw him and threw the ball. He barely managed to catch it.

"THREE!" Remers and Kern yelled out.

Pratzsky held the ball awkwardly and looked for blue eleven. Ditch was staggering up from her push-ups. He called out and threw the ball. She lurched for it, but missed, swore, then went after it. Blue eleven was the soccer kick. He ran to it.

Seckie was on her last one—a devilish thing they called 'the hyena'. It was simply really, a co-ordination exercise involving point-steps to the front, side, and back, while the arms were lifted up, out, and down. But it had to be done in front of the weight-lifting mirror. Five times in a row right. Under normal circumstances, that was enough to defeat even those who *could* walk and talk at the same time. Placed at the end of a run, the hyena usually reduced everyone to a hyperventilating amoeba with three arms and no legs.

Ditch, hearing Seckie's shrieks of laughter, knew she was doing the hyena. She began to chuckle too, sneaking glances, as she started red thirteen. Mats—two front rolls, three back rolls, a headstand, and a cartwheel. She loved to see the guys at this one. Men simply could not do cartwheels.

And Pratzsky, Pratzsky had the ball again. Ditch had thrown it back just before she started on the mats. He couldn't throw it to Seckie and the rules allowed only one throwback, so he was stuck with it for his last one, blue fifteen: sponge ball bowling. It was a silly station, he thought. Probably Seckie's idea. He threw the ball, and watched as it bounced crazily on a zig zag course that missed the 'pins' entirely. He concentrated on another throw—and missed again. He looked around then—Ditch was nowhere to be seen, but he had to finish before Seckie. He tried again.

Seckie, with an idiotic leer on her face, was doing the hyena in slow motion. Very slow motion. Taking an interminable amount of time between each toe point and arm lift. Forward right with up. Forward left with out. This was her fifth time. Out right with down. She was not going to mess it up again. Out left with up. Back right with out. She paused, thinking hard. Back left … with down. Yes! She lunged dramatically for her bell and beat it to death, stopping her time clock but good.

Pratzsky knew then that Seckie had finished. He threw the stupid sponge ball again—and missed again. Should he pass and call it quits? His time couldn't be that good anyway, Seckie and Ditch were both done already. Then again, maybe yellow and red were fast runs this time. And he liked the idea of being able to do it over and over until he succeeded. But enough was enough. He glanced to the end of the gym. The four of them—Seckie, Ditch, Remers, and that new guy, Kern— were chorus-lined in front of the mirror doing 'I'm a little teapot'. He shook his head. Two throws later, he got a strike. Yes! He trotted to where the others were and half-heartedly rang his bell.

"Oops," Ditch said as she went to stop her clock, looking at Pratzsky, daring his anger.

"Geez!" he spat. These guys were no fun at all. He thought he had beaten Ditch's time on the red run when he'd drawn it the time before— now he'd never know. Shit.

"Blue is a tough course," he said, leaning forward to rest his hands on his knees. But his chest was no longer heaving.

"They're *all* tough, Pratzsky," Ditch said, loping her arm around Seckie's shoulders and grinning. "We make 'em *all* tough."

Then she clicked in to the 'old school' subtext underlying Pratzsky's comment, and realized that her response had, within that framework, detracted from his effort, devalued his performance. "But you done good, Pratz," she tried to repair. "Was it fun?"

He ignored her question. It was either trivial or patronizing. Or both.

"Remember the course we set up last summer, out at Ditch's place?" Remers reminded Kern of 'Mrs. Poole' on *The Hogan Family*—bubbling in spirit as well as body.

"*Oh* yeah," Seckie said, with a rueful grin. "I couldn't move for a week after."

"What was the course like?" Kern asked. He had just joined—in fact, he had just been hired by the company. Expecting a squash round-robin or a baseball team, he found 'mittsiball' instead. It shouldn't have surprised him though. The company operated on flex-time and had an in-house daycare too.

"Well," Ditch began, "first of all, we made it part scavenger hunt. You had to look for the coloured markers that would tell you what and where your next station was."

"Stupid idea," Pratzsky commented. The others laughed, and Kern waited for an explanation.

"Pratz spent the better part of an hour looking for 'red two'," Remers volunteered, then burst out giggling again with the others. "It was up a tree!"

"At least when I hid the blue markers, I used a bit a common sense!"

"Anyway," Remers brushed past what was obviously still a sore point, "we included a bush hike, a bit of a rock climb—"

"And a swim in the lake—"

"And three cannonballs off the dock," Seckie remembered.

"To which some of us added Tarzan yells." Ditch laughed at Seckie.

"And ..."

Pratzsky left the group to tally up the scores. If he didn't do it, it didn't get done. Actually there had been a bit of discussion at the outset about whether or not to even keep score. He was called old-fashioned and conservative. Well, maybe he was. But what was the point if you didn't keep score? He checked the individual times against the point grid. Then he subtracted points for every station passed on (allowed, but only after trying it for thirty seconds). Points were added to the individual scores for every successful ball pass; unsuccessful passes and put downs (putting the ball down to do a station) lost you points. At the end of the play, you added up all your points from the best five or six runs, however many the person with the least runs did. His time for the blue run was 14:26—not bad, he thought. But then he had nothing to compare it with. Maybe Kern would get blue this time. He took the sticks off the table and moved back to the chatting group.

"I'm surprised you didn't make one of the stations 'catch a chipmunk'!" Kern was enjoying himself.

The others looked at each other.

"Write that down," Seckie said to Ditch.

Pratzsky interrupted then, to recite the scores, but Kern was the only one to pay attention. The others knew better. A stunning individual time could be wiped out if no passes were made. So much depended on who your trio was, and that was everchanging, depending on the luck of the draw. That's what made it so neat, so interesting. Mittsiball was a test of adaptability and versatility, as well as a test of strength, flexibility, co-ordination, speed, and endurance. Optimum scores were the result of optimum co-operation between optimum individuals.

"So," Pratzsky said loudly, "are we ready to go again?"

"Okay!"

"Yup!"

Pratzsky held out his fist, holding the five 'pick up sticks'. Remers and Kern had to go this time, so they picked first. Remers' stick was yellow-tipped and the one Kern had pulled out wasn't painted.

"Pick again," Seckie told him. He did so and got the red run. Then Remers took the remaining three sticks and held them out to Seckie, Ditch, and Pratzsky. Seckie pulled the blue.

"Whew," Ditch breathed, "my shoulders could use the rest. Whose idea was red eight, nine, and ten, by the way?" No one answered. "Rope climbing?"

"Oh, I suggested that. Why?" Kern felt uneasy, embarrassed—he was new to setting the runs.

"Monkey bars?"

"Mine," Seckie grinned and dangled her arms like an ape.

"And push-ups—Pratzsky?" He nodded.

"Well," Ditch pointed out the problem, "they're all in a row!" Then she explained to Kern, "Usually we're a little more co-ordinated in our creations."

"Well, it's too late now," Pratzsky said impatiently. "Let's go!"

"No," Seckie said, "we can change it."

"I'm doing red this time. It's okay with me …" Kern was unsure, but he thought he felt some personal politics here.

"Okay," Remers said, smoothing it over, "then let the games begin!"

She quickly dinged her bell to start her clock and was off. She knew she wasn't really getting a headstart, but so what? Kern started his clock and ran onto the gym floor after her, looking for red one. Seckie remembered to take the playball with her, but then from the middle of the gym, she had to call back to Ditch, laughing, "What colour am I?"

"Blue!" Pratzsky yelled.

As soon as she finished her first station, bench hopping, Seckie passed the ball to Remers, who was always watching, always waiting. Pratzsky and Ditch called out "ONE!" She moved on to blue two. It was a joy to play with Remers. You could throw her the ball even when she was doing the tires and she'd catch it—if you aimed well—without missing a beat. Seckie remembered one time, on a course much like this one, Remers had made a perfect pass—perfect timing, perfect aim: Ditch had caught it in mid-air coming down from a lay-up. Then almost without thinking, Ditch landed, took two steps as if going for another lay-up, and passed it to her. She was on the monkey bars and with a reflex action, caught it with her feet. She finished the bars, flicked the ball from her feet to her hands as she jumped down, and passed it back to Remers who was just coming out of the tunnel. Remers had to make a small grab for it but, always alert, caught it. The whole sequence was incredible, so smooth ... it was as if they'd rehearsed it. Seckie heard "TWO!" then, and looked to see Remers casually climbing over a hurdle, humming a little tune. Trot trot trot—climb. Trot trot trot—climb. She looked for Kern. He must be crawling through the tunnel with the ball. She carried on to blue five.

But it got that way after a while if you played with the same people. You got to know their strengths and weaknesses. For instance, Seckie knew you never ever passed at Ditch when she was moving backwards. Actually moving forwards was kind of a risk too—that's why that one play was so fantastic—but in between stations, Ditch always looked and was always ready.

Playing on the same course made a big difference too. Not only did you get to know where the lulls were in any given run, you also got to know where the runs intersected—physically, so the pass would be more of a hand-off, but also temporally. "THREE!" she caught the pass from Kern.

For instance, she thought as she approached the bicycle, chances are that while I'm on blue nine, the red player will also be on nine, but the yellow player will be on eleven or twelve. Some stations always take longer than others, that's just the way this course went. Before she climbed onto the bicycle, she passed the ball to Remers, who was of course expecting it. No one liked to pedal with a ball in their hands. "FOUR!" So at that point, a pass between red and blue would be difficult, because red was monkey bars. But yellow could pass to blue—

as long as the aim was accurate, because blue couldn't move—"FIVE!"—and blue could then pass back. No, she couldn't, Seckie remembered in time—only one passback was allowed.

However, the red player, Kern, was only at five. He knew he was going slowly. He kept looking for the ball to come flying through the air and hit him on the head. He didn't want to look ridiculous. He laughed then. So what did he look like standing in a line with three other adults doing 'I'm a little teapot'? He saw Seckie on the bicycle with the ball, and he held out his hands. Seckie threw it to him. "SIX!" Ditch and Pratzsky yelled, cheering.

It was hard though, to find that balance—between the attention, the energy used on individual performance and that used on group performance. There was a point at which both maximized. Kern recalled, as he ran up and down the bleachers, that as a child he was fascinated with standing on the teeter-totter in the middle, just so, so that both ends were off the ground the same amount. As an adult, he saw himself running along the splintered board first to one end so the other flew high in the air, then back along to the other end so the first end was off the ground. If you had only your own rhythm to consider, he thought, either way achieved a balance. But group efforts had a rhythm of their own. You had to be ready to maximize your attention to the group at that moment when individual input would maximize the group's performance. No point in being ready to pass the ball when no one else could catch it. He wondered how long Seckie, Ditch, and Remers had played mittsiball. How long did it take to find that balance, that timing?

Before he started the dreaded eight, nine, ten sequence, he had to throw the ball. Remers was closest. "SEVEN!" Was that a lot of passing? The group before had only what, four passes? "EIGHT!" Remers had passed it to Seckie. He scrambled up the rope and back down. Then he jumped up to hang from the monkey bars. He started across, right, left, right … his arms were sore, but really, it wasn't too bad. He dropped right into the push-ups. A little slow, but do-able. And as soon as he got up, he saw the ball coming. He reached for it, fumbled, recovered. All right! He heard cheers—and "NINE!"—and felt rather pleased with himself.

Then he heard Remers laughing. The hyena? Had to be. He glanced over. It was. She looked like a drunken octopus. Heading for red eleven, he saw Seckie on the sidelines. Done already? Must be. She was so fast! He'd have to carry the ball for the rest. That meant he'd have to set it down for red thirteen—and lose points—or do a one-handed cartwheel. Yeah right.

He heard a bell. Again and again. That must be Remers, done with the hyena. We should put a gong there instead, he thought. Cymbals, at least. Well here goes. He tucked the ball under his arm and did two front rolls. More or less. Three back rolls? He tried one. Splat. He tried again. No way. Inspiration hit: he put the ball under his shirt and tucked his shirt into his shorts. Can a pregnant man do back rolls, a headstand, and a cartwheel? Ditch, Seckie, Remers, and Pratzsky were watching to see. Yes to the back rolls! Yes to the headstand! And— YES! A cartwheel, by a man, with a belly out to here! They cheered and hooted. He bowed before trotting over and ceremoniously ringing his bell.

"Nine passes," Ditch complimented the threesome. "Way to go!" She nudged Seckie and nodded to Kern. "Wait till this guy tries the course out at my place."

"I look forward to it," Kern smiled, exhilarated.

Seckie had the sticks in her hand. She offered them to Ditch and Pratzsky first. Ditch pulled blue and Pratzsky pulled red. Yellow went to Kern.

"I have to go again?" Actually, he wanted to. In spite of and because of the sweat running down his face.

"Now we'll see what you're really made of," Pratzsky slapped him on the back. He looked out at the expanse of the gym, tracing the red run.

Seckie gratefully sat down beside Remers to watch the play. She had done three in a row a few times. It was hard. But fun hard. She liked mittsiball. Rumour had it that the originator had named the game after her puppy; it didn't surprise her, if Mittsi had been anything like her own dog. She had a terrier spaniel, a little over a year old, with a black fluffy coat dipped in caramel, and wisps sticking out all over that made her look inquisitive, reckless, and of course, just plain cute. Seckie often watched her play 'tug of war' with one of her many friends: as soon as the other dog let go, she'd dangle the leather strip or whatever (she was resourceful when it came to toys) right under its nose, nudging it, insisting it grab on again and play some more. She had no concept of win/lose. 'Playing ball' meant wait for the throw, race after it, pounce on it, and bring it back prancing-oh-so-pleased-with-herself, to wait again, race after it again, pounce on it again, and bring it back again, and again, and again ... She never kept score, and only fatigue determined when the game was over. She played for the hell of it. It was as simple as that.

Seckie laughed then as she stretched out her legs, remembering just this morning. She had happened to look out the window and see her: sprinting around the tall pines, dodging in and out as if they were a slalom course, pausing every now and then to lean on her forepaws, rump in the air—panting, and giggling at the trees.

The School Board

"Len!" His father called angrily toward his bedroom again. "Len!"

"What!" He'd been disturbed from sleep.

"It's eight o'clock. Doesn't the school shuttle come by at eight-thirty?" He was standing at the doorway now, in his heavy coat, gloves, and hat, lunch pail in hand. He looked with disdain at his sixteen-year-old son, still lying in bed.

"I'm not going to the school," Len muttered and rolled over.

"I won't have you skipping school again!"

"There's no such thing as skipping anymore. Attendance isn't compulsory anymore, remember? I don't have to go to school," he said saucily.

"You don't have to go to school. What, you know everything there is to know?" Though he had to admit that much of what his son was supposed to have been learning before was good for nothing. But things had changed, hadn't they?

"You can't make me," Len delivered the bottom line.

"Then have the driveway shovelled, the house dusted and vacuumed, the dishes done—and fix the strapping in the crawlspace, the insulation is falling down. And the woodstove can be emptied, you know where the ashes go." He stopped a moment. "That's hardly eight hours' work, so why don't you make up a batch of chili and freeze it—"

"Don't know how." He'd discovered a refuge in ignorance. It released him of responsibility.

"You know how to read, don't you? Use the cookbook!" He was shouting. "And try to fix the snowmobile—"

"Can't. I tried. I don't know how to fix it." He was sullen.

"I guess you're fired from that job then."

"And I'm not gonna do all that other stuff either, I'm not your slave." He put his hands behind his head and stared at his father.

"And I'm not yours!" He was enraged. "You expect me to buy your food and make it? Want me to serve it to you too, on a silver platter maybe?" He hit the doorframe. "If you don't fix the snowmobile, I guess you can't use it. And if you don't make the chili, you won't be eating it. Unless of course you can pay me for it. Got a job?" he chided. Then he turned away in disgust. How many times had they been through this? "I don't have time for— You better learn one thing: you get nothing for nothing!" He stood there in silence for a moment, expecting a response. Then he looked at his watch. "Shit, I'll be late for work again," he glared at his son. "You'll get me fired and *then* where will we be, what will we eat, eh?"

Len heard his father slam the door. The truck started and after a minute or so, he heard him drive away. He relaxed back into his bed, but he felt no victory. What *would* he do all day? He was tired of watching tv. He had no way of getting to Bud's house. Bastard, he thought, why didn't *you* fix the snowmobile? You could've done it last night, at least then I could go see my friends. He felt like a prisoner. Bet he did that on purpose. He wondered if that was child abuse. His dad was keeping him from, what did they call it, 'social development'? Maybe he'd mention it tonight. Fuck, he looked outside at the snow blowing. Too cold to even try to hitch a ride.

He got out of bed then and walked into the kitchen. He took a bottle of juice from the fridge, then went to their telephone/computer in the corner. He sat down at the little table and called up the School

Board. It was easier than looking it up in the newspaper. He could turn on the tv to the School Board channel, but the tv was in the other room. And anyway, it was one of the free bulletin boards. He scanned the screen … there were tons of courses. Many were offered at the school, but there were a lot at workplaces and people's houses. The school shuttle went everywhere. Accounting, biochemistry, broadcasting, cake decorating, Canadian geography, computer skills, electrical I, English language, English literature, French language, French literature, Greek history, Latin. He couldn't believe people were really interested in this crap. He sure as hell wasn't. He fast forwarded. Snorkelling, snowmobile repair—he stopped. He punched up that course. It had started last week. Figures. He punched up a screen showing everything starting today. He crossed it with things needing no prerequisite. He was left with Intro Science I. Yeah right. Well shit, there was nothing else to do. He looked at his watch. Eight-twenty-five. Fuck. He washed up a bit, put on some clothes, and ran out to the shuttle stop.

Ivanya Summer moved through the hall full of students. They were of all ages and all of every other variable you could think of as well. She was heading toward Room 107, one of the science rooms. It was the first day of the term. There were three four-month terms now. Three times a year, she could feel this first-day-of-school feeling. Used to be this excitement was part anxiety: would it be a good class? Or would so-and-so be in it, and so-and-so.

Several students were waiting at the door, smiling and eager. She chatted with them as she opened up the room, and five minutes later, at nine o'clock, she began the class.

Not with taking attendance. It didn't matter who was and who wasn't here. There was no punishment for absence, no bonus for presence. If a student wasn't here, maybe they wouldn't master the topic of the day (or the topic of the next day, given how most knowledge and skill developed). And if they were here, they could count on her help. It was a simple as that, now.

Now, attendance at school was compulsory only until the person was literate and numerate. There were a few standard tests to be taken, by anyone at any time—read the newspaper, write a letter to your government rep, have a mock conversation with a mock doctor to explain what the problem is and to understand what to do about it, fill out your income tax return—and then you were, if you wanted to be, through with school.

She began to hand out the texts and schedule for Intro Science I. As an intro course, it had no prerequisite. However, this was rare. Most courses required certain courses to be taken prior; or in lieu of that, adequate performance was required on a test measuring the skills and knowledge that would've been acquired in those prerequisite courses. The class met for an hour every day and every two or three days there was a new topic: how does a plane stay up in the air, why do leaves change colour, how does aspirin work, why do male dogs lift their leg when they pee. And on and on.

As she began to talk a bit about the schedule, the door opened and a young man, about sixteen, sauntered in. He walked across the front of the room with a smirk on his face.

She continued, "So that's what we're—"

"Where am I supposed to sit?" he accused her. She thought it best to ignore his attitude.

"There's an empty desk over there," she pointed.

"Oh." He walked over toward it.

"So that's what we're going—" A loud scrape of chair along floor interrupted her. She looked angrily at him. He shrugged, exaggerating apology, blaming the desk.

"What we're going to do in the—"

"Hey Axelrod," Len had seen someone he knew across the room. "Do you have a pen I can borrow?" he called out loudly, then looked at the teacher, daring her.

For a moment, it was like so many of her classes used to be. Too many of her classes. There was always one or two, or five or six, or ten or fifteen kids who couldn't care less about the lesson, who did not want to be there. And they were unable to amuse themselves quietly. Sure you could kick them out, send them to the vice-principal's office. And lay yourself open to the charge of 'inability to control the class' or 'poor classroom discipline'. And anyway, that was an option only if there was one such student. There were, after all, a limited number of chairs in the vice-principal's office. And yours was not by any means the only class with uninterested students. Sometimes she'd send them out into the hall, to mellow out or cool off or whatever—hoping to make headway talking to the student one-on-one and away from the gaze of the rest of the class. But more often than not, the student just took off, and *she'd* be the one in the vice-principal's office because one of her students was found wandering the halls and didn't she know that she was legally responsible for each and every one of her students for the duration of that period? Besides, as the vice-principal may point out, if the student isn't in your class, she or he can't learn. And, as you'd be reminded, it was your duty to teach them.

And so would begin every teacher's understanding of the many roles to be played. Teacher as prison guard and teacher as drill sergeant. Or for the more hopeful, or at least the more creative (the more energetic?), there was teacher as entertainer, teacher as class clown. Whatever, everyone soon realized it all boiled down to teacher as fool. After you tried to entice, coax, and trick them into learning, you coerced them. When that didn't work, you bribed them—with marks usually, but also with no homework or a spare on Friday. Eventually that didn't work either: students stopped caring about marks, stopped doing any homework, and stopped showing up on Friday.

Eventually, someone somewhere realized that you can lead a horse to water but you can't force it to drink. No matter how hard you whip it, no matter how attractive you make the water—if it isn't thirsty, it won't drink.

She turned her attention back to Len, who had begun to drum loudly on his desk. "You don't want to be here, do you? You don't want to find out why—," she looked at the schedule she had just passed out, "why chickens run around after their heads have been cut off."

"Nope. I don't. Hey Axelrod, do you?" The boy on the other side of the room smiled nervously and was silent.

"Then please leave." It was a simple as that, now. And if it wasn't, she could phone for an escort.

For a moment, Len forgot that things were different. "What, you're not sending me to the office? No detention?"

"No. The only consequence of your behaviour is losing the privilege of attending this class; and the only consequence of that is, I suppose, that you'll have to learn the material—that is, if you want to learn it— on your own, without my help."

"Think I want your help?"

"Obviously not. So you shouldn't have come in the first place." She paused and asked the question she could now ask. "Why *did* you come?"

He got up so violently the chair clattered backwards to the floor. He walked out and slammed the door.

Used to be, Ivanya realized, I'd now consider him *my* failure: my failure to interest him in science, my failure to motivate him to want to learn about science, my failure to help him find the real cause of his anger. (Did I forget teacher as psychologist and teacher as social worker?)

But now—it suddenly occurred to her—how *do* you get the horse to drink? Make it thirsty. Deprive it of water. And in essence, that's what this new system did. It wasn't pouring water down their throats six hours a day, five days a week; it wasn't even holding out a glass. It wasn't withholding it either, but the deprivation would be there just the same. Len would be ignorant. He would be without knowledge, without skill. Whether or not he would become thirsty would depend on whether or not he recognized knowledge and skill to be a necessity. It was easier with water. Water was tangible, and drinking some directly and immediately alleviated thirst.

She handed out a diagram of a chicken's insides. Then she put an overhead of the same diagram onto the projector, and with a blue felt pen she traced the path of the nervous system, explaining as she went along.

"So the chicken continues to feel things after its head has been chopped off?" someone asked.

"Do our nervous systems work the same way?" someone else asked.

She fielded their questions, then gave them some time to field hers.

And people were accustomed to direct and immediate effects, she continued her previous line of thought. Cause wasn't understood otherwise. 'Deferred gratification' was an oxymoron these days. What with songs being no longer than three minutes, hour-long tv shows having three story lines and any one scene lasting no more than two minutes, ads being thirty seconds, sentences in the newspaper being ten words or less—no wonder their attention spans had become so short— if you didn't get it right away, you didn't get it. 'Trying' supposed time. 'Persistence' an eternity. And it's like they have no conception of time: no memory of the past, no plans for the future—this moment is all that exists. They're like children, she realized.

For a while she had thought that if the courses were valuable, they wouldn't have to trick, coerce, or bribe. But their value was years away.

Too far away to be perceived. Or their value lie in an 'if-then': if you want to be a forest ranger, then you have to learn plant biology; if you want a high school diploma, then you have to get thirty credits. Too indirect to be noticed.

Fuck! What a bitch! So now what, Len thought as wandered down the hall. It used to be a fine thing to get kicked out, to be sent to the v.p.'s office. First it was initiation, then it was worth so many points. But now— He leaned against some lockers, then slid to the floor. He could sit here all day. No, he couldn't. Someone would notice him, call the cops, and he'd be picked up for loitering. Okay, so he could sit somewhere else all day, he could go to the washroom. He remembered how many teachers he'd fooled with that one. "Miss?" What teacher would say no and risk him pissing all over the floor. He would too, they knew it. So they'd say sure, making some comment about interrupting the class, or controlling his bladder, or asking why he didn't go during the ten-minute break between classes. "Didn't have time—had to go to my locker and get my books for this class and it's way over at the other end of the school and my last class—" Once a teacher actually suggested he get the books for *both* morning classes and carry them all morning with him so he wouldn't have to go to his locker between classes. But no, even the washroom was out, now. There was no one there.

She listened to their answers to her questions. There were some very good hypotheses.

"All right, I like what I'm hearing. If you'll turn to page ten in your text, you'll find more information on nervous systems. Take a few minutes now to check out the theories we've just heard with the facts."

The seeds for change had been planted mostly by teachers who had been on exchange programs, especially in developing countries, and by night school teachers. They were the ones who got things going. Ivanya supposed that they were the ones to whom the existing state of affairs was most clearly a farce. A ridiculous, pathetic, definitely unsatisfactory farce. Many simply could not return to regular day school teaching in this country, it filled them with such disgust—after having experienced an educational context in which the students *want* to learn and *try very hard* to do so, after being able to be simply and magnificently teach as teacher.

The changeover was simple actually. Ten percent of the Ministry of Defence budget was transferred to the Ministry of Education—with no strings attached to the number of students in attendance. So suddenly there was no need to force anyone to be anywhere to learn anything. Suddenly a lot of administrators had time—which, along with that $1.2 billion, was used to run schools round the year and round the clock. All the fringe 'alternative' learning programs burst into growth, and an extensive learning network developed. Whenever and wherever someone decided they wanted to learn something, it was relatively easy to get (back) into the school system. And, with money left over, a joint program was established with municipal recreation and police departments, to set up youth drop-in centres next to all major school buildings.

She began to circulate among the students, stopping here and there to help them help themselves.

The result was astounding. Smaller classes. Full of people who wanted to be there, people who wanted to learn. 'Discipline problems' became non-existent. And though it was too early to really tell, Ivanya thought the students were changing. They weren't coerced anymore to be there or to learn a certain subject, so they were gradually losing the habit of resistance they had acquired. It freed up a lot of energy. Energy they used to spend on refusing, in a thousand different ways, to do, now they could spend on doing. The habit of participation, even of co-operation, was beginning to develop. Learning became active, instead of passive—not because of the strategies taught in teachers' college to make it so (strategies used all along, but to no avail), but because without compulsion, presence became a matter of choice. And to choose to attend became to choose to participate. Then, not only did they become participants, they became initiators: once you were concerned with the possibility of doing (as opposed to the problem of not doing), the decision of *what* to do became possible.

Everyone was over at the drop-in probably. It was next to the school and had a gym, several lounges, food and drink machines. A lot of kids hung out there. All day. He had. For four months actually. But you can play only so much basketball and so much euchre day after day, eight hours a day. Even the talk got boring. When you got right down to it, no one had much of anything to say.

That was another thing, Ivanya thought, returning to her desk. Decision-making. When something is mandatory, there is, in essence, no choice to be made. So it used to be that students weren't accustomed to making decisions. Oh sure, they could decide whether or not to do their homework, they could even decide what courses to take. But most students didn't care about such things, and a decision without real interest in the possibilities as well as in the outcome isn't really a decision. Besides, the consequences were seldom really experienced. If they didn't learn the material, so what? They still survived, still had food, water, and shelter. They still got jobs. (It didn't matter what you knew, it mattered what you looked like—put on a suit and tie for the interview—we taught them well.) And usually they still passed, what with teachers inflating grades to give students a feeling of success (in the hope that then they'd be motivated) and department heads inflating grades to make the school look good (see, our students are accomplished; see, we're successful teachers). So they learned/we taught them that they can succeed without trying, without achieving—that they can get something for nothing.

The feeling of success should've come directly from the achievement, not from the mark put on it. Part of the problem was, again, the perceived worthlessness of the task and hence its achievement (I can solve a quadratic equation, whoopeedoo). Marks—that was the other part of the problem. Like money, they were an intermediary that became an end. Most people don't want jobs, they want money. Because there are lots of jobs, i.e., lots of things to do, and yet the unemployed complain. Because they're 'unpaid', not because they're 'unemployed'. And students didn't want to learn, they wanted marks. Everyone forgot that the money was *for* the job done, that the mark was *for* the skill or knowledge mastered. And so cheating, like theft, became logical. You can steal money, but you can't steal a completed task; you can cheat to get a mark, but you can't cheat to acquire a skill or knowledge.

But now that they can make a decision, about something that really matters to them (shall I go to school or not), and now that they will experience the consequence of that decision, Ivanya thought that the students were feeling more responsible for their own lives, for their own happiness. If they weren't learning, now their first thought was that it was *their* fault—I wasn't listening carefully enough or I didn't do the assignment. And if they were bored, it was *their* problem—I should drop this course and find one I *am* interested in. And, she hoped, after that responsibility for self would come a feeling of responsibility for others, maybe even for the world. Once they did for themselves (instead of waiting for the school, the teacher, to do for them, to them), they might start thinking of doing for others.

It was painfully clear now. When you're not forced to be part of, not coerced to co-operate, you will do so more often, and more willingly. And so you will learn. And with knowledge comes power. Power to—

So he could wait for the next shuttle and go home. And do what, watch tv? Certainly not that list his dad had yelled at him.

Maybe he'd raise a little hell, he thought. Kick in some lockers, write on the walls. What for, he suddenly wondered. 'Cause I'm fucking angry! He knocked over a recycle bin.

What are you fucking angry about? There ain't fucking nothing to do! He could go to student services. They had to help him find something to do. That was their job. Yeah sure. He remembered going to student services a few months ago.

"So, Len, how can we help you?"

"I don't know, you want me to tell you how to do your job?" he'd asked without making eye contact.

"Are you having trouble with one of your classes, your teachers … ? Maybe you need advice on a course of study that leads somewhere?"

"I'm not taking any courses."

"Okay, then let's start there. Do you want to?"

"I don't know."

"Well, what interests you?"

"I don't know."

"There's nothing that you enjoy doing?"

"No, not really." He paused. "Driving around on my snowmobile."

"Ah, okay, good. We have a snowmobile repair course." She punched up the School Board to find the listing and get the details.

"*Driving around* on it, not *fixing* it." Stupid bitch.

"Okay. If I could find someone into snowmobile racing—"

"I don't want to race." Are you crazy?

"Okay. So you like driving around on your snowmobile. Unfortunately, I don't think anyone will pay you for that—wait a minute … There's probably some snowmobile patrol force …" She turned with excitement to the computer and in a few seconds she was reading from the screen, "You'd need to get your first aid and—"

"I don't want to do no first aid."

"Why not?"

He shrugged his shoulders. "Just don't."

"But if it meant you could—" she stopped. The patrol force was probably better off without him then.

"Okay, I assume you want a job though, eventually. Or do you already have a source of income?"

"What?"

"Do you know someone who's willing to—to 'keep' you for the rest of your life: to pay your rent, buy your food … or at least pay your taxes if you intend to build your own house and grow your own food."

He was silent.

"Do you know how to build a house and how to grow food?"

What was she asking that for?

"Well, do you?" She was getting exasperated.

"Do I what?" He was getting angry.

"Know someone who will buy you a snowmobile and keep its tank full!"

"No!"

"Then you need a job, right?" She had punched up the Job Board. "What kind of job would you like?"

"One that pays good."

"Okay … doctors get paid well."

He looked at her and laughed as if to say 'Yeah, right, me a doctor.'

"You don't want to become a doctor?"

He looked at her again. Boy, was she dumb.

"I don't like school. Doctors have to go to school for a long time, don't they?"

"Yes, before they apprentice. They need to know the names and functions of all the parts of the body … Can you think of a better way to learn all of that than by going to school?"

Len got up to leave.

"Wait a minute," she'd gone too far. "You know you don't have to 'go to school', right? I mean you can learn at home by correspondence on your computer. Or you can learn at someone else's home. We have lots of off-site possibilities. And then there are apprenticeships—learning at a workplace—what used to be called 'co-op'."

He sat back down.

"Let's take a look …" She scanned the job board, reading aloud listings at random. As expected, every single position required some kind of certificate of skill or diploma of knowledge. "Anything here of interest to you?"

He wasn't even looking at the screen she'd turned toward him.

"It seems you're going to need a certificate or diploma in *something* … Let's go through the School Board, and see if we can't find something you're interested in."

So they began to go through the School Board listings. Acrylic painting, archeology, architecture, auto mechanics. She paused there hopefully. No response. Biology, blueprinting, ceramics, chemistry, drafting.

"Maybe we're going at this wrong. Maybe there isn't anything we can offer you."

He grinned sarcastically. "You got that right."

"Maybe I should be asking what you can offer us."

He was silent.

"Do you have any skill you can pass on to others? Do you have any ability your community needs?"

"No."

"Well, you've got two arms and two legs, a sixteen-year-old body, there's a task force cleaning up the rubble from that—"

"You mean be a volunteer?" The word was repugnant to him. "No fucking way."

She turned with a sigh back to the computer screen. Electronics, engineering, English language, English literature, flooring, floristry, forestry, guitar. He grunted.

"You're interested in music? Would you like to learn how to play guitar?"

"Already did. I took that class for *three* days and I still can't play anything."

"I see. You want something you can learn and do in one day."

"Yeah."

"And get paid."

"Yeah." Now she was cooking.

"I have just the thing then."

She'd lined up a seven-hour apprenticeship on an assembly line leading to a job that paid minimum wage. When the apprentices got a break for lunch, he'd left.

It was ten o'clock, the class was over.

"Try a few of the problems on page eighteen, and for tomorrow, come up with one good question about nerves," she smiled, "or chickens." The students left, chatting happily to each other.

Sure, there were still casualties of the system. Some chose not to go to school and discovered later that, for some things, it was easier to learn when young. And some were like that boy. Hard core cases. Oh well, she knew, he'd've been a casualty in the old system as well. And he would've taken a few others down with him—some easily influenced friends, a teacher dying of burn-out. She knew his type. Interested in nothing. Scornful of everything. Always arrived late and unprepared. That is, when he arrived—he skipped school more often than not. Never did any homework. Expected nevertheless to learn. And insisted on passing. Probably never been to a library. At least, not on his own. Hopeless, she almost thought. But she knew that some kids loafed for two, even three years before thinking 'Hey—.'

She sat at her desk a while longer, making a few notes on the students she had just seen. Throughout the course she'd enter comments into their computer file, notes on their achievements and their level of understanding of the material. The students would also add material to their file, mostly copies of work they had done. Then whenever the student requested it, a multidisciplinary jury would review his or her file and decide which, if any, certificates or diplomas could be awarded, and with what standing.

Why *did* he come? Good question. He didn't know. Shit. Maybe I'll check the School Board again, there was one in the main foyer. See what's starting next week. Or maybe I'll go to the library— Where *is* the fucking library?

New and Improved

Jack was sitting in the living room. It was evening. He wasn't reading the paper. He wasn't watching tv. He was playing ping pong. Back and forth, back and forth. The game had been going on in his mind for several weeks. Every now and then a point would be made by one side. Then the other side scored a good point.

Aaron appeared in the doorway with two glasses of iced water, a slice of lemon in one, a slice of lime in the other. He looked at Jack. Jack in his grey hair and blue jeans. "Having second thoughts?"

"And third and fourth and fifth," Jack smiled. Aaron came into the room, handed Jack the lime water, then sat in his favourite chair. It looked like a piece of lawn furniture. Jack was sitting in the middle of the couch.

"I'm fifty years old, Aaron. I've been in advertising since I was twenty."

Aaron waited for him to continue, watching the droplets of condensation trickle from his glass onto his track pants.

"I'm disposable! I don't think a day goes by without Ross getting a resume and portfolio from some new young guy." He paused, then backed up a minute. "Portfolio? What am I saying? These guys have a handle on computer graphics and synthesizer effects and—they come with videos, not portfolios." He took a long drink.

"If it bombs, you don't really think they'll fire you, do you? You've struck out before."

"Yes, but there doesn't seem to be as much room for error these days." He had moved to the edge of the couch.

"Geez," Aaron reflected, staring at the hands that held his glass. "What's the point of getting to our age if we can't rest secure in our seniority?"

"I know. But that doesn't seem to count anymore. Now you're only as good as your last ad. And *it's* only as good as the sales it generates."

"So they'd put you out on the street? Take your pension right out from under you?"

"Well no, I guess they wouldn't actually fire me," he waved his glass vaguely in the air then gazed at the slice of lime. Its pulpy green belly. "They'd just ask if I wouldn't like to retire early." He took another long drink, finishing it.

"Couldn't you—"

"No, no other agency would hire me. And what else would I do? What else *could* I do? Who would hire a fifty-year old man? For what?"

Aaron thought for a minute, then began to say something, then hesitated. Then he said it anyway. "I know this isn't the point, but— Don't worry about the money. Jack, you know we can both live on my income. Indefinitely."

"You're right, that's not the point. But I'm glad you said it anyway. Thanks."

Aaron knew Jack would resume in a minute. He took as swallow of his lemon water.

"You know what twenty from fifty leaves?"

Aaron was used to Jack's rhetorical questions.

"Thirty. Thirty years of my life have been spent manipulating and deceiving. I'm tired of it, Aaron. No, I'm *sick* of it, that's what I am." He put his glass on the coffee table in front of the couch and settled back a bit. "What I'm *tired* of is the triviality. For thirty years, I've been wrapped up in how clean X gets your clothes, what Y tastes like exactly, and whether Z moves fast enough. You know," he sat forward again and toyed with his glass, "it doesn't make me proud, Aaron."

"Wait a minute Jack, you've come up with some of the best ads in the industry!" Aaron protested. "It takes talent to create in half a minute something that lasts days, weeks, months—something memorable—"

"Hiroshima was memorable!" He flung out his hand and knocked over his empty glass.

Jack's anger startled Aaron. But he accepted it quickly and went on from there. "You're not killing people, Jack—"

"Aren't I?" Jack glared at Aaron. "Treat someone like a moron for long enough, and sure as hell they'll turn into one! My ads— All ads have made people brain dead!"

"All right!" he agreed. "So go with it then!"

Jack retreated quickly. "They'll say I'm all dried up, they'll say I have no new ideas left—"

"But you're proposing a whole new concept: 'political purchasing'. No," he reconsidered, "'power purchasing'." He smiled. "It's more '80s. Actually," he added, "what you're exposing is pretty new too. Hasn't been done before, has it?"

"No. So you really think I should go with it? I still have the other version—"

"I think you should do what you have to do." Aaron finished his drink and got up to leave. "You have to live with yourself." At the doorway he turned then, and grinned at Jack. "But whatever *you* can live with is what *I* can live with."

Jack smiled. And nodded.

His meeting with National Motors was at ten o'clock. At ten to, he walked through the doors of their head office. He knew where he was going, but as a courtesy he stopped to inform the receptionist.

"Jack Patrice, Best Ads Agency."

She looked at her master list, but couldn't find it.

"That's P-a-t-r-i-c-e?" She picked up her telephone.

"Yes … There it is." He had been scanning the list upside down. "BAA," he smiled wryly.

"Oh, yes, thank you," she saw it near the top. "You're expected at ten in the boardroom, Mr. Patrice. Ninth floor, left off the elevator."

"Thank you."

He walked across the marble floor of the foyer to the elevator. He pressed 'up' and waited. A man in a suit and tie, carrying a slim attaché case. Very much like the man who stood here several times before over the last twenty or twenty-five years. Only now he was— No, not jaded— And he wasn't less excited. But it was a different kind of excitement. He was more … fearful? Was that it?

He felt sad to recognize that. He wished he felt eager, as he had on those other occasions. He saw the other man striding along with this great new ad that was going to make the entire industry sit up and take notice! But he didn't feel like striding. He felt like tiptoeing. He also felt like stomping, damn it, the time was right! In fact, this ad was long overdue, thirty years overdue.

The elevator doors opened. He strode into it, pushed 'nine', and watched the doors close. Presentation is everything, he reminded himself as he stood with his shoulders back. The ad deserves it.

The doors opened, he stepped off the elevator, and turned left. As he rounded the corner, he almost bumped into someone.

"Hey, Jack!" Joe Porowski clapped him on the shoulder. "How are you? Go on ahead, we're almost ready. I'll be back in a second. Men's room," he explained, "—again," he added grimly. This would be Joe's last year with National Motors. Actually, three years ago was supposed to be his last year, but somehow he had stayed on. And on.

Arthur Kent was waiting for Jack at the doorway. He held out his hand, "Jack, good to see you again. How's everything?"

"Just fine, Arthur, thanks." He and Arthur had known each other since they'd both started out, in the sixties. Arthur had sat through every one of Jack's presentations, and though their paths had no real need to cross, they'd kept loosely in touch over the years, playing the odd game of golf, having lunch every now and then. Had their circles intersected naturally for some reason, they probably would've been close friends.

"Let me introduce you to the others," he said to Jack, then motioned in turn to several people seated around the table. "Marta Barnes, Phil Rose, Ben Llewellyn, and Satoh Awai you know already, and Michel Beaucage. And Joe—"

"Here I am, here I am," Joe came into the room.

"Yes, we bumped into each other in the hall," Jack smiled.

"Well then, we're all here!" Arthur looked at his watch, then at Jack. "Shall we get started?"

"Sure," Jack replied. He went to the head of the table. After setting his attaché case on the table, he opened it and took out seven copies of a single typewritten page. He passed them around, and while they read it, he waited.

Joe mumbled his to himself. "'Frankly, National Motors' new Falcon is about the same as the old one. The ride still isn't as smooth or as quiet as with some other cars. And it still doesn't look very sexy. We've improved the exhaust system a bit, but it'll still be the first thing needing repair and replacement. But our parts are relatively inexpensive.'" He looked up at Jack with surprise. Perhaps with horror. Then continued.

"'Ten other cars will get you from zero to sixty in less time, but few others will get you from sixty to zero as quickly.

"'Falcon's fuel consumption rate is 9.5 litres per one hundred kilometres.

"'The Auto Association rates Falcon's transmission and steering better than average, and its electrical system worse than average. Consumer Reports say the cooling system is fair to satisfactory, and the engine is excellent. 87.2% of Falcon owners are 'very satisfied'.

"'National Motors gives 3.4% of its pre-tax earnings to charities—this is about 1% more than most. We have one woman and two minority members in top management. We are not involved in nuclear weapons related work—in fact, we have no military contracts at all. And we have our own environment officer now, whose job is to monitor both our products and our production.

"'If you'd like any other information before deciding whether or not to buy National Motors, whether or not to buy a Falcon, call us at 1-800-471-2122.'"

Phil Rose broke the silence that followed Joe's mumbling. "What's this?" There was disbelief, and possibly disdain, in his voice.

Jack looked at him. He was one of those young guys he had told Aaron about last night. He forgot to mention their arrogance.

"Maybe," Arthur intercepted, trying to hide his own reaction, "since this is such a new—such a change in direction for you—for all of us—perhaps you could tell us where you're coming from on this one, Jack—then we'll get into any discussion."

"Sure, Arthur," he answered. But he was still fluctuating between polite diplomacy and impassioned diatribe, between soft sell and hard sell. He noticed his hands were trembling. As in 'Fear and —'? Or as in '— with rage'? He didn't know. He looked again at Phil. Cocky, sitting back in his chair, hands clasped behind his head, waiting expectantly. For a moment, Jack wondered if he'd been like that.

Then he laughed. The quick glance to thirty years ago made him see the thirty years. He'd had a career. He didn't have much to lose now. He felt he could finally risk integrity.

"You hired me to advertise your product," he said. "That's what I'm doing. I'm advertising your product. It's not a lifestyle, it's a car."

"But you're supposed to make our product look good," Ben Llewellyn spoke up. He was an older 'establishment' type—most of the time.

"No, *you're* supposed to make a good product," Jack almost interrupted. "I'm just telling it like it is in this one."

"What about the visuals?" Michel Beaucage asked, in a carefully neutral tone. "What did you have in mind for a magazine or television spot?"

"Still of a Falcon—car, voice over," Jack answered. "Very simple, very forthright."

Michel smiled at his answer.

"That's it?" Phil asked, yes with disdain.

"That's it. No anorexic females with blow-job mouths in this one."

Phil coloured.

Someone chuckled.

"But you make it sound like the new Falcon isn't—well—isn't very new," Joe complained.

"Well it isn't really, is it? Frankly, I don't know why National Motors keeps coming out with a new model each year. Hasn't anyone ever stopped to figure out how much that's costing you? From the engineers' salaries, to the factory reassemblage, to the advertising ... No other product line changes its design every single year. It doesn't make sense!"

"And what's the 1-800 number?" Joe seemed not to have listened to Jack's response. "Do we have a 1-800 number?" he turned to Arthur.

"No," Jack intercepted. "It's an idea—to make the company more accessible, more answerable, to its customers."

"That's what our salesmen are for!"

Marta Barnes spoke up next. "Why the bits at the end about women, minorities, the environment?" She looked like part of the cast for a show called *The Young and Professional*.

"I think it's important that people know where your company stands on issues like that. It lets people put their money where their mouths are." Jack hoped she was more than a token presence.

Michel turned to Marta. "Did you know that one of our competitors has become so involved in military products that its automobiles are virtually a public relations sideline?"

"No, I didn't." She looked at him, then thought about what he'd said.

"I like the idea," Michel smiled at Jack.

Jack tried not to look grateful.

"Our investments are not matters for public knowledge," Ben differed. "We have our shareholders' privacy to protect. Is it any of *my* business what you do with *your* money?" he asked Jack.

"It might be if your money *becomes* my money. You may not want me to have it if you know what I'm going to do with it."

No one seemed to have anything more to say.

"Any other questions or comments before we take a vote? Satoh?" Satoh hadn't voiced a response.

"It's an interesting strategy, Jack—"

"No, it's not meant as a 'strategy'. Don't you see? That's exactly what I'm trying *not* to do—be 'strategic'! This isn't some game we play, to win or lose—"

"Oh yes it is, Jack," Joe spoke up. "And until now, you've been a pretty good player. I don't understand why you're heading for the bench now!"

"Maybe he's just trying to change the rules a bit," Marta defended him.

"Or recognizing that yours isn't the only game in town," Michel's tone bordered on hostile.

Accurately gauging the tension, Arthur spoke up. "Shall we vote?" He nodded to Jack that he could sit down, the discussion was over.

Phil spoke first, like a sprinter held too long at the starting block. "No hype, no excitement, too dull, too boring," he ticked items off a list, a report card, "it won't catch people's attention." He looked up. "Mr. Patrice seems to have forgotten all of the basic principles of advertising. I say no."

Michel countered immediately. "I like it. I'm tired of being lied to and being treated like a child, manipulated like some mindless idiot. And it's refreshing to hear about what's really important."

"Joe?" Arthur asked.

"Sorry, Jack. I think I hear what you're saying and I might even agree with you, but it's too risky. We have a business to run here. Can't take the chance."

Jack thought about responding, but Michel beat him to it.

"What chance? Are you saying we can't afford the truth? If we can't stand behind our products, then what the hell are we doing here?"

"If you don't know, maybe you shouldn't be here!" Phil said coolly.

"Ben?" Arthur ignored them and tried to get on with the vote.

"Well, I guess as one of those two 'minority' people, I'm supposed to support your idea, but, sorry Jack. I just don't. We can't tell them our exhaust system is no good!"

"They already know," Michel stated flatly.

"Well maybe so, but it still makes us look bad. And I can't go along with the other stuff. I know you want to jump on the anti-nuclear and pro-environment bandwagons but—"

"I don't think they're bandwagons" Jack said stiffly. "Don't *you* remember the peace marches? And Pollution Probe's been around for as long as *I* can remember."

"Well that may be so, but we're selling cars here, Jack, and people are buying cars—and personal politics has nothing to do with either of them."

"Marta?"

"I'll back anything that doesn't use 'anorexic females with blow-job mouths'," she grinned. "I support Mr. Patrice's ad."

"And Satoh?"

"Well, you know, it's different enough it might work. I say yes, let's give it a try."

Arthur stalled. It was three for, three against. This didn't happen often.

Joe turned to him. "Arthur?" They were all looking at him, waiting.

"Well," he started slowly, "I don't know much about marketing strategies," he looked at Phil. "And I must admit I haven't thought a whole lot about the nuclear thing or the environment," he looked at the others. "And I don't even drive a Falcon," he chuckled a little. Then he knew where he stood. "But I've known Jack for over twenty years—I do know him. I respect him and I trust him. I vote yes."

Several months later, the ad was out.

Jack was sitting at his desk at Best Ads, going through some paper work. His phone rang.

"Jack Patrice speaking."

"Hello. My name is Mrs. Schnawbernechty," he recognized Aaron's falsetto. "Are you the young fellow who did that new ad for National Motors?"

"Yes ma'am, I am," he played along.

"Well I just wanted to tell you that I think it's—what's the word you young people use nowadays—groovy? I think your ad is real groovy. We need a lot more like it. That must've taken a lot of courage, did it?"

"Well—"

"I applaud you, Jack Patrice."

"Thank you, Mrs. Schnawbernechty," he laughed over the name.

"By the way, young man, are you free for dinner?"

"Well, yes I am!"

"Fine. I'll pick you up at—what time do they let you off work there?"

"Five o'clock, ma'am."

"Just fine. I'll be there at five."

"I look forward to it."

"Too-doo-loo!"

"Bye, Mrs, Schnawbernechty, and—" Jack paused, touched, "thanks for calling."

He hung up the receiver, grinning.

Just then the mail person came by. She parked her cart beside his desk. "Are you the one who did that ad about that car's bad exhaust system—"

He sighed. Not the transmission, not the steering, not the engine. When all was said and done, the bad exhaust system was remembered.

"—and the nuclear weapons thing?"

He brightened a bit. "Yes, I am."

"Then you're the 'whom' this concerns." She handed him a letter.

He smiled. A letter too? He expected it to be from Mrs. Schnawbernechty. But it wasn't. It was a photocopy of a letter to National Motors from a Noreen Anson. It read simply: 'To whom it may concern, Any company that supports the environment is a company I support.' He smiled. He beamed.

Two more letters came in the afternoon's mail run: 'It's so refreshing to be treated like a thinking, feeling, adult human being—able to receive information and make choices. Thank you.' Jack laughed. This was great.

He read the other one: 'I'm not sure I agree with your stand on nuclear arms, but I do agree that it's more important than how fast the ketchup comes out of the bottle.'

Jack leaned back in his chair. He thought about writing to these people. To thank them for thanking him. His intercom buzzed.

"Mr. Patrice?"

"Yes?"

"Bonzo Burgers wants to talk to you. Line one."

The Sexual Evolution

Delaine and Antonio were sitting at a worktable in the corner of their research room. It was eight o'clock in the morning. They were both drinking coffee with the intensity of anticipation. They were waiting for Shoshonee, the third member of their team. They were waiting for the results of a study that had taken, so far, over a year of the Institute's resources.

They had begun by spending two months soaking themselves in the existing literature: they found out about everything that had already been done that had anything to do with what they were planning to do. Then they got a grip on the current stuff, the relevant studies-in-progress. Then they took a month to select their sample. Then another month to revise it, as various schools, companies, municipalities, and other groups said they'd be unable to participate. Nevertheless, in the end, the beginning, they had almost 10,000 subjects representing the full spectra of age, gender, income, education, occupation, culture, philosophy, etc., etc., etc. It had taken another two months to prepare the questionnaires. Then over six months of mailing them out, receiving them back, coding them, and entering them into their computer base. The next step, analysis, had been left to the stats whiz of their group, Shoshonee. She'd been spending upwards of ten hours a day almost every day of the past month collating the data, cross-referencing everything, checking for relationships, tossing the numbers into every possible configuration to see what patterns existed …

There was nothing compelling them to rush except the excitement of being near the end, of taking the last turn in a long journey—of finally finding out where you've gotten yourself to. Shoshonee expected to be able to tell them today.

Seconds after the noon whistle blew, Ed was in the lunchroom, one hand barely managing to hold a huge salami-ham-and-pickle sandwich, the other flipping through a well-smudged copy of *Studies Illustrated*. An article on sex caught his eye, and he stopped to read a bit of it till the others came in.

Suddenly Shoshonee flung open the door and burst into the room. "We've done it!" she cried out triumphantly, waving a floppy disk in her hand.

"We have significant results?!" Antonio half-asked, half-echoed, his body relaxing with obvious relief.

"Oh—that too," she said, as she switched on one of the computers and loaded the disk.

"That *too?*" Delaine asked. "What did *you* mean we've done?"

She turned to them and with the gravity of a great announcement, said "We, as a species, have evolved away from intercourse as sex!"

"What?" they both exclaimed.

She nodded vigorously with her back to them as she punched at the keys of the computer. Then she pointed to the screen. "No one is having sexual intercourse anymore!"

"No one?" It was hard to believe. They crowded around the computer to look at the statistics she had called up.

"Well, only two percent of the population. The deviants," she grinned at them.

Antonio slowly found his way back to his chair. He sat down. He didn't know what he found harder to believe: the significance—98% of anything would make the *world*, never mind the Institute, stand up and take notice; or the results themselves—no more sexual intercourse?

"Not as recreational sex," Shoshonee answered, and he realized then that he had muttered his disbelief aloud. "When people want to reproduce," she punched up another set of numbers, "they engage in sexual intercourse. Otherwise," she smiled, "penile-vaginal penetration slash enclosure is a habit of the past."

"Wow." Delaine had also returned to the table to sit down.

"So—Tony, you'll prepare the briefs? We can get an article in the journals right away, and of course a preliminary final report to the Institute," she whirled to Delaine then, "and Dell, do you want to start writing the book while I put together the discussion of our findings?" She smiled at her stunned research partners. She had already passed through this shock of discovery, several hours ago.

"Book?" Then Dell seemed to snap out of it—or into it. "Of course I want to! Write the book. Masters and Johnson, move over!" She looked about for pen and paper as if to begin that very instant. "What are we going to call it?"

"Well, I remember an article called 'The Sixties: The Sexual Revolution'. It changed my life," Shoshonee grinned. "I thought we'd call this one 'The Nineties: The Sexual Evolution'."

"I love it!" Dell looked over at Tony then, and punched him on the shoulder. "Wake up! We did it!"

"No," he said slowly, and gestured vaguely at the world, "*they* did it." Shoshonee nodded in agreement with his implied praise and sat down at the table to join them.

"We're dinosaurs, Bill," Ed called out to the greying man who had entered the lunchroom, "about to become extinct. You still fuck your wife?"

"Actually no. I never did fuck my wife," Bill said, sitting on the bench at the long table. "We made love," he smiled.

"Ed fucks his wife," said a third man, who had come in just behind Bill and had heard the question. "But only when she lets him." He paused. "Too much hassle otherwise, right Ed?"

"You mother-fucker," he grinned.

"Hey Tom, you still diddling your wife?"

"What kind of question is that to ask a man?" He half-turned to acknowledge that Beth was behind him.

"Well, are you?"

"Well, no. Not since we had Keel."

"Fifteen years?" Ed couldn't believe it.

"We didn't want more than three kids, and the pill gave her headaches and the IUD made her bleed and well, hell, sex isn't *that* important!" He started to eat his lunch.

"Not that important!" Ed snickered and nudged the guy beside him, who smiled uncertainly.

"So what are they doing instead?" Dell asked. Tony glanced at her, grinning a bit. He had recovered somewhat. "I mean," she amended, "I know what the possibilities are, I want to know what the realities are."

"Well," Shoshonee bounced up and skipped over to the computer again. She punched up another screen. "A lot of attention to touching and stroking the erogenous zones," she read out, "breasts, nipples, of both sexes, the chest, neck, thighs, wrists, legs, back—"

"What's *not* an erogenous zone?" Tony smiled.

"A lot of sound—music—" Shoshonee stopped. "Remember the new age movement? Music for relaxation, for healing, and so on? The science of psychoacoustics really took off then. Remember all those studies about the effect of sound on the human organism, its biorhythms, etc."

"Yeah, 'Heavy metal increases one's blood pressure.' I could've told them that," Tony grinned.

"Well, there are tons of cassettes and stuff available now. 'Sensual sound' they call it: some focus on rhythm, some on timbre—"

"Are you saying that because of *that,* our sexual practices changed?" Dell asked.

"I don't know. Do we know which came first?"

"More likely the supply encouraged the demand," Tony suggested.

"But if they didn't think the market was there—"

"And dancing is making a comeback," Shoshonee was leaping ahead. "Have you seen what 'Dirty Dancing' has grown into?"

"Hang on!' Dell was trying to take notes, to put all of this into some kind of sense later.

"It's almost like a regression, isn't it?" Tony thought aloud. "When sex was taboo, all of these other things became very sexy."

"No, this is definitely a step forward—"

"But Shon, he has a point. Sex—sexual intercourse—*has* become taboo again. For physical reasons this time though, not moral ones."

Dell made a few more notes as Shoshonee continued, referring back to the computer. "And there's use of scent—"

"That's understandable. Just look at the perfume and candle/incense industry."

"And use of light—"

"Sounds like a lot of people are into a very carefully composed environment ..."

"Use of props and costume," she continued scanning the screens, "what you wear, how you put it on, take it off ... Gloves are big—"

"I thought 'performing' was on the way out," Tony commented.

"This doesn't sound like performing," Dell said. "It sounds like pleasing, exploring the full range, the whole realm of sexual pleasure ..."

"A lot more talking—" Shoshonee continued.

"How do you explain that?" Dell asked. "It used to be you said nothing at all."

"Or sweet nothings," Tony amended.

"Hm. Remember when sexual assault really came out into the open?" Shoshonee said. "The courts were full of hearings and trials and the clincher always seemed to be consent. We realized that the normal *modus operandi* was for the male to approach physically before knowing whether or not the female was receptive, before actual consent—an uncanny similarity to rape—"

"Even animals have it straightened out better than that, don't they?" Dell commented.

"So maybe flirtation, maybe even 'foreplay'—though I don't think that term has any meaning anymore—maybe flirtation became, almost for legal reasons, very verbal: it wasn't just eye contact and subtle touches, it became much clearer, it became 'I want to be sexual with you' or 'Do you want to be sexual with me?'"

"A far cry from 'Shall I compare thee to a summer's day?'" Tony lamented.

"That's right," Dell agreed. "Remember that pop song, 'Do You Want?'?"

"Ah—Barry White and Donna Summers." He began to hack it, switching voices with each line, "'Do you want to touch, do you want to touch me, do you want to feel, to feel me, feel me touch you, to feel you touch my—'"

"No, it wasn't them," Dell cut into his performance, laughing, "but you're right, it could have been—twenty years later."

"I wonder if homosexuality didn't also contribute to opening up the repertoire. A lot of same sex couples weren't into penetration. We should read the literature again on homosexual practices—especially lesbian, we may find a lot there ..." Shon scribbled the idea onto her note pad.

"What else?" she looked up. "What other reasons can we suggest to explain our findings?"

"Besides the obvious one you mean?"

"What about you, Beth?"

"What about me? Am I still fucking my wife, is that your question of the day, Ed?"

The others laughed.

"When I was growing up," she continued, "we had this thing called AIDS. Ever hear of it, Ed? It's for the most part genital-sexually transmitted. And it's for the most part, fatal. So I said—," she looked straight at him, "Fuck it!" The others hooted and hollered.

"You mean you never—" one of them asked.

She shook her head. "Never."

Ed blinked but then said, "Yeah but you're just a woman, your needs aren't—"

"Me neither," a youngish man in the corner spoke up. "Same reason."

"Don't you feel—unfulfilled?" Ed grinned at Beth, ignoring the man.

"I'm working at a ten dollar an hour job with the likes of you, and you ask me if I don't feel unfulfilled?" It was her turn to grin, and a few of the men chuckled.

"You know what I mean—"

"Yeah, he means unful-*filled*," someone snickered.

"Listen, the movies I can roll in my head are better than any show any of you could put on for me," she looked straight at Ed again, "even twenty-five years ago!"

They gave her applause on that one.

"Don't forget," Dell suggested, "there were a few years in there ...

remember that vicious backlash? For a while, *all* abortions were illegal and there was talk of making contraception illegal again too—"

"Yeah," Shoshonee agreed, "that was surely an incentive to explore alternatives."

"The ascent of the male ego," Tony offered.

"What?"

"Well, it used to hang down between our legs?" He grinned.

"Hey Stud! Did you read this article in *Studies Illustrated* yet?" Two younger men had entered. One was especially handsome, and a bit of a mascot for the crew of mostly older, faded and jaded men. He caught the magazine Ed had tossed at him and skimmed the article, reading certain sentences aloud. "'The act of sex' is now more properly called 'the art of sex' ... 98% of the people who 'have sex' say it does not include sexual intercourse ... They report a wide range of activities, including ...'" He started grinning as he read, to himself now, the most popular repertoire.

"Well?" Ed interrupted his pleasure.

"Well, what?"

"Is it true? Guys like you—you're still—aren'tcha?"

"Ed, when 'guys like me' are out on the town, we're out engaging in—" he smiled as he quoted, "'the art of sex', not making babies." He unscrewed a bottle of pop and grinned at Beth. Not for the first time.

Ed raised his eyes at the other young man.

"Hey," he answered the implied question, "you're talking prehistoric. I'm a 'sexual artist' too," he laughed with delight at the term, "not a baby machine!"

Ed looked disappointed, but he bounced back and nudged Bill. "Us old dinosaurs will just have to keep them fires burning—"

"Speak for yourself, Ed."

160

"What?" There was a fear in his voice as he turned to face Bill.

"I found out long ago, Vera likes a lot of other stuff better than that, so ..." Seeing Ed's face crumple into what looked like pain, he added quickly, "Angela may be different—"

"Who's talking about Angela?" Ed roared, too loudly.

The Great Jump-Off

"And that," the old man pointed to the next photograph in the album, "that is your great-grand-aunt Carol." The little girl tucked beside him on the rocking chair looked carefully at the picture.

"Now there's a person you would've liked, Larah," the young man sitting across the room said.

"Is ze dead now?"

"Yes, she is," the old man answered, and she accepted it in the same way she accepted sunsets.

"Was ze your sib?" she asked.

The first time he'd heard her use 'ze', he'd thought she was just having trouble with the 'sh', but then he heard 'sib' instead of the gender-specific 'brother' or 'sister'. He'd managed to get used to 'chair' instead of 'chairman' and 'firefighter' instead of 'fireman', but not much more. The massive language overhaul had occurred when he was well past fifty. And, like his parents who'd used 'miles per hour' and 'pounds per square inch' until the day they'd died, he figured he'd be saying 'he' and 'she' and 'his' and 'hers' till the day *he* died.

"Great-grand-za?" He felt her tiny hand on his cheek; he must've dozed off.

"Yes, yes she was. My sibling. She was Carol Sagan." He smiled at the memory.

"Have you told Jeth about 'The Great Jump-Off'?" It was a scratchy voice.

"No," the young man turned to the other person sitting in the sun room, one of his grand-za's friends, "he hasn't." He turned back to his grand-za, curious. "What was 'The Great Jump-Off'?"

"Was it a game?" the little girl asked. It was the hope of all puppies.

"No," he smiled, "it was much more serious than a game. Do you know what religion is?"

Larah shook her head.

"Well, it used to be that a lot of people believed in something they called 'God'. Something they could never see or touch or—"

"Like 'Santa Claus'? Kids used to believe in Santa Claus. They said he was an old man with a white beard and if you were good he gave you a reward at the end of the year."

"No Easter bunny either?" he looked sadly over her head to his grandson.

Jeth shook his head. "But that's not to say there are no surprises in her life. Every now and then she gets a secret gift. Or gives one."

"But the magic—"

"There's enough *real* magic in the world, grand-za. Right now it's fireflies. Two months ago it was prisms. Before that, bubbles."

Larah tugged at her great-grand-father's sleeve. She hadn't followed that part of their conversation. "So was God like Santa Claus?"

"Yes. Actually God was a lot like Santa Claus." A Santa Claus for adults, who didn't want to grow up, he added to himself.

"When did they all jump off?"

The old man laughed. That was well-put, he thought.

"Well, first there was 'The Face-Off'. That's an old television show your great-grand-aunt appeared on from time to time. It was sort of a one-on-one debate, a discussion of important ideas and issues ..."

"Quiet on the set, please."

Ann Randall focussed on the camera. She was relaxed with

confidence, excited with anticipation. This was going to be a good show—one of the best, she thought, in her five years as host.

Sitting on one side of the table was Carol Sagan. She knew Carol from university. They had both studied philosophy. Carol was perfect for *Face-Off*: articulate in a clear and simple way, fearless but not vicious, intensely passionate but not fanatic.

Facing her was Marion Eplett. She was a strong woman, firm in her views, reasonably intelligent, and very representative of 'the people at large'.

Carol represented the atheist view, though of course the name for it had disappeared at a rate in direct proportion to its rise in popularity. Marion was a theist: it was a word heard more and more, where before she'd be called—when called anything—a Catholic, or a Presbyterian, or a Methodist, or Jewish—whatever.

The face-off, Ann thought, was going to be between knowledge and belief, reason and faith.

"Welcome to this week's 'Face-Off'," Ann said suddenly, on cue. "This week on our show we have ..." It took only a moment to introduce the participants. Carol began immediately.

"Marion, why do you believe in a god as the creator of the universe and not, for instance, a purple platypus?"

"Well, because that's ridiculous. To believe in a purple platypus doesn't make—" Marion stopped.

"It doesn't make sense? But belief is independent of reason. What does it matter if it makes sense or not? I can list a thousand things you believe that don't make sense."

Ann repressed the impulse to smile.

"So, again, why don't you believe that 'The Great Big Purple Platypus' created the world?"

"Well because it's just not true. God—"

"Not *true?* So you're *not* talking faith, you're talking *knowledge?* You *know?* You can *prove* 'God' exists then?"

"Oh yes!" Marion said with relief. "Theologians have been proving God's existence for ages! For example, everything must come from *somewhere*—"

"Says who?" Carol asked.

Ann leaned back then. They were off and running and would need no assistance from her.

"Well— Logic, I guess—"

"Reason?"

"Yes, okay, reason," she said cautiously. "And that's the basis of proof for God's existence. He's the something that created everything," she finished uncertainly.

"And who created God?"

"No one. He's omnipotent. He created himself."

"So you suspend the very logic that got you to God in order to explain God: everything has to have a cause, therefore God—but then suddenly everything *doesn't* have to have a cause, therefore God!"

"Is that a problem?"

"It's inconsistent! It's illogical!"

"God is exempt from your logic. He transcends reason!"

"But it's not *him* that's transcending it, it's *you! You're* the one who's saying 'Now I'll use logic, now I won't.' That's why your 'proof' is invalid. It's unreasonable."

"But as I said, and Kierkegaard will back me up on this, it doesn't *have* to be reasonable."

"Then why not believe in The Great Big Purple Platypus instead?"

"What?"

"Why isn't The Great Big Purple Platypus the being that created everything including itself?"

"Well, I suppose God could take the form of a purple platypus, but there's no support for the existence of anything like that."

"There is for God's?"

"Oh yes, we have reason to believe—"

"So you're going to use your reason again? You seem to use it when it pleases you and toss it out when it leads to an unfavourable conclusion," Carol's tone was not as cruel as it could have been.

Marion ignored her. "*The Bible*, the Dead Sea Scrolls, relics, first person testimonies—"

"*The Bible?* What about the contradictions in *The Bible?*"

"I beg your pardon?"

"Well, how do you decide which stories to believe when there are two different ones?"

"Such as?"

"Genesis, for starters. There are two versions about the creation of man and woman. Which do you believe and why?" Marion was silent.

"And what about the Apocrypha—all the stories that were decided by somebody at some time to be left out? There's one that says God has no gender. Why do you believe the 'He' version instead?"

"Well, I'm sure there was good reason to omit ..." she trailed off. "Look, I'm not saying there aren't weak spots in my faith. But surely it's better to believe in something than in nothing at all! Are *you* saying it's better to be *pagans!*"

"That's interesting," Carol commented. "You use the word 'pagan' as if to suggest someone primitive, someone unenlightened. I use the word 'Christian' in the same way. However," she went on, "you misunderstand. I'm not saying I believe in nothing. I— Maybe I am," she retracted. "I don't need to *believe* in anything, because I *know*. I believe, if you will, in knowledge, in reason."

"But a godless world? I can't imagine!" Marion was horrified.

"I can." It was said simply, without apology.

"We'll take a commercial break now," Ann broke in with impeccable timing, "but we'll be right back," she smiled at the camera.

She offered glasses of water to her two guests; the intermission was brief and silent.

"But don't you see?" Marion was eager to resume, as soon as the break was over. "With no sense of right or wrong—"

"Theists don't have a monopoly on morality," Carol interrupted. "Ethics do not have to depend on a god."

"Well without God, how would you know what's right and wrong?"

"*We* would determine that."

"On what basis?"

"How about justice? 'It is good to treat everyone equally.'" Of course it wasn't that easy, Carol knew. 'Justice' would have to be defined, and to treat everyone 'equally' may not be 'just'. But if Marion didn't want to pursue that aspect …

"And what's to stop someone from being bad?"

"What stops them now, the fear of God's punishment?"

"Well …"

"Do you mean to say that the only reason you're good is because you want to get to heaven? Isn't that, by your *own* standards, wrong, because of its self-interest?"

Marion paused for a moment. Then she asked triumphantly, "Can *you* sit there and tell me right now what's just?"

"No." Carol admitted it calmly. "It's not that black and white. If you want simple answers, go back to your catechism. The world is full of grey complexities. But as intelligent and sensitive adults, I think we can arrive at the answers we need."

"What about Sundays?" Marion changed the topic. "You'll be taking away family time—don't you believe in the sanctity of the family?"

Carol stared at her blankly. The connections weren't particularly strong, so it took a while for her to see them.

"Well," she said after a moment, "you're forgetting about flextime. Parents can simply choose a workshift that parallels their kids' school shift. But surely that's—"

"And are you advocating a world without prayer?" Marion had interpreted Carol's slowness as a sign that victory was near. She intensified her questioning.

"Prayer?! *Yes*, I'm advocating a world without prayer! It's easy to talk to a god that doesn't talk back. But it's more effective to talk to the people you share life with."

"And what about the children?"

"What about them?" Carol asked.

"Who will we turn to for guidance in this heathen world of yours?"

"To ourselves. We can—"

"You deem mere mortals to be better—," she could hardly say it, "better than God?"

"Yes, I do."

Marion was white. "You will not trust in God?" It was incomprehensible.

"No, I will not. To trust in 'God' shows pretty poor self-esteem, don't you think? Why can't *we* just *figure out* what's in our best interests? Look at all the remarkable—dare I say miraculous—things we've done. Can you name one feat of God's in the last thousand years that rivals the telephone? The electrical outlet? The pain killer?"

"But all the telephones and electrical outlets in the world won't save us."

"And God will? I'll put my money on my reason any time. Maybe not electrical outlets. Maybe, instead, a method of re-oxygenating the oceans, maybe a worldwide ban on all nuclear weapons, maybe—" she broke off suddenly.

When she resumed, her tone had changed, ever so slightly. "It's your faith versus my reason. My reason tells me that if I jump off a cliff attached to a hang-glider that is built to a specific design, determined by rational thought, I'll land safely at the bottom. Your faith tells you to trust in God: jump off the same cliff without the glider—*He'll* save you, right? Because He transcends the knowledge of science, the reason of logic. Am I correct?"

"Yes."

"Then let's do it." She meant it.

Ann was shocked, and she moved to intervene.

"Okay," Marion had answered.

Time was up. The program was over. Ann recovered, thanked her guests, and delivered the sign-off. Then as soon as the camera was off, and Marion had left the set, wordlessly, Ann turned to her friend.

"Are you crazy? She'll kill herself!"

"Yes. I know that. And you know that. She believes differently."

"Or knows it too and accepts it. You made it hard to refuse."

"I'm not responsible for her decision."

"But your very participation in a stunt like this will be as good as approving it!"

"But I do!" Carol assured her. "Or I never would have suggested it. Frankly, I admire anyone who acts in accordance with their opinions."

They were ushered off the set; Ann directed Carol to a quiet corner where they could continue their conversation.

"Look Ann, it's time to stop being polite to theists. It's time to stop smiling amused, as if they're children with harmless lollipops. They're *not*! There are large numbers of people who believe that any interference in the course of events is to mess with 'The Divine Plan'."

"But—"

"They think anti-nuclear activists and environmentalists are doing the devil's work, for God's sake! They're *for* nuclear war because such global devastation fits the Biblical description of the end of the world!"

Ann was surprised, and shocked, and not completely convinced. Carol pressed on.

"Some of these people hold positions of political and economic power. They're dangerous, Ann. And our silence only condones their doctrine of inferiority and impotence. Look," she pleaded, which was unusual for her, "we can't afford to have half the human race walking around muttering how unworthy they are, 'waiting for Godot' to save them, living in the meantime in a state of fearful dependence." She paused, then finished grimly. "Quite the contrary, Ann. We need all the competence our species can muster."

"So did it happen? Did they have 'The Great Jump-Off?'" Jeth was fascinated and horrified at the same time by his grand-za's story.

"Well, a lot of people were against it. Theists and atheists alike. Many, like Ann, thought it was a bit drastic. And some said it was just plain silly. The theists cried out 'Who are we to presume, to demand that God prove himself how and when and where we want? God doesn't need proof!' But then Carol cried back, 'Then neither does The Purple Platypus, and it's His will that all theists die!' That really threw them for a loop," he chuckled.

"And some tried to accuse her—'Those who need proof are weak in spirit!' 'But strong in mind!' she answered."

Jeth waited, the question still in his eyes.

"Yes," the old man finally said. "They had 'The Great Jump-Off'. Carol and Marion. Then Carol and Bob. Then Carol and— Well, you get the picture ..."

The media had provided ample notice of the event. So when September 14 arrived, a bright, sunny day, crowds began to gather at the precipice as early as eight a.m. The Jump-Off was to take place at one-thirty. The chosen spot was one of the more accessible cliffs in the Tremblant ski range. It had a lot of flat space on top and a lot of flat space at the bottom—and nothing in between.

Ann's network had pressured Carol to retract her challenge, to pull out of the event. Their ratings had risen since that particular episode of *Face-Off*, but they were worried about legal proceedings after the event—a worry presuming a death. And although initially in agreement with her network, Ann, after reading a fair amount of literature on the activities of numerous religious groups, their rituals, education, investments, etc., reached full support of Carol's action. When she made her support vocal, the network fired her. With profuse apologies.

The two of them were at the top now, Carol making a thorough check of her hang-glider and harness, Ann fending off the media to allow her to do so.

"No, we're not part of any group per se, we're here as individuals."

"Because we know that it's better to act according to reason than according to faith. Knowledge, not belief, is the way out of our global tailspin."

Carol smiled drily at her choice of word.

"Yes, that's true. And we agree with you. But we're past the naiveté of the independent: what people do or do not do on their own *does* affect the people next door—even if they're not in positions of political or economic power. 'It's none of your business' is almost always a lie, now."

About thirty feet away, Marion was surrounded by a group of people on their knees praying.

"Dear God, help me in this, my hour of need. As you have before," Marion remembered the first time she went rock-climbing, a frayed rope nearly cost her life, but God had been with her, "so I believe You shall do again. I place my fear in Your hands, Almighty God. I come to you,

Our Father, as Your loving and dutiful child. I trust Your guidance, Your will shall be done.

"Hail Mary, Mother of God, pray for me, a sinner. By the powers of your intercession, grant me …"

A man near the edge of the circle, next to someone wearing a yarmulke, suddenly stopped murmuring his rosary. He lifted his bowed head. An image had suddenly come to mind. Peter Pan? 'If you close your eyes and wish hard enough—and clap your hands three times'? He was *not* a child. He stood up slowly and turned to Carol and her hang-glider, and in a moment he saw that she was right. He might've called it a revelation. He didn't. He knew it was simply understanding. He left the prayer circle.

A megaphoned voice announced that it was time for 'The Great Jump-Off. Carol walked over to Marion. They hugged each other. Then they stood at a spot some distance from the edge. Carol fastened herself onto the hang-glider. Marion whispered one last prayer. They took a few running steps and jumped off the cliff.

No one spoke. No one moved. No one went to the edge to see what had happened. Everyone knew.

When Ann arrived at the bottom, Carol was slowly packing the hang-glider harness into its travelling case. The waiting ambulance had already taken Marion's body away. There was nothing to say. Carol's face said it all: not quite triumph, not quite horror.

"Teach me how to hang glide," Ann said, "and I'll do the next one."

Carol looked at her, held her gaze for a moment, then nodded.

"So there was—a next one?" Jeth asked.

"Oh yes," the old man remembered, "and a next one, and a next one. For some, Marion's death didn't change a thing. She became a martyr: 'The Lord works in wondrous ways', 'We don't always understand why

He does what He does', 'We must just accept it', 'He knows best'. Or she became an unfortunate: 'Her faith wasn't strong enough', 'God punished her for the sin of pride'. And so another would try. And another. Trying hard to ignore the thought that if he believed *his* faith was strong enough, he was guilty of the same sin. It was a catch 22: How can you think you've been 'chosen' while maintaining humility?" He paused to be sure Jeth appreciated the dilemma, then continued.

"But for others, Marion's death did make a difference. It became painfully clear to them what a scurry of ass-covering they had done all their lives. They became angry at the spot they'd been put in—by Carol, by God—by reason, by belief."

"And *did* it make a difference? Overall, I mean?" Jeth wanted to know.

"Who really knows?" he looked not at his grandson, but at a spot in the air between them. "People changed, but it could've been for a number of reasons. Things got worse—much worse—you've probably studied the food, water, and oxygen rationing in history class."

"Yeah. It's incredible—that people let it go so far."

The old man looked at his grandson. He had far too much to say to that one, and nothing at all.

"People became less accepting, less passive," he tried to describe the change. "I don't know, it seems there was less apathy, less lethargy. They stopped waiting for something to happen, they stopped thinking that they'd wake up one day and everything would be better, I guess. They stopped trusting in whatever it was they had trusted in to make it better.

"I suppose that could've been the result of a loss of faith: when there is no Divine Plan, when there is no *God* whose will will be done, then I guess people figure out pretty quick you have to make your *own* plan, carry out your own will. If you ask me, I've always thought 'God's will be done' was just a high and mighty 'que sera sera', a religious laissez-faire, an excuse for laziness. It was plain and simple passing the buck.

174

"Along with that," he resumed, "came a crushing sense of responsibility. For the past, the present, and the future. Everyone knew *it was our fault; we* were to blame—not a god, not a devil. And since there wasn't going to be any knight in shining armour—no god in blazing glory—come rescue us, well ..."

He tried to summarize. "There was a lot more co-operation, it seems to me, after 'The Great Jump-Off'. Co-operation with each other to find a way out—"

"I wonder if the concept of an afterlife had anything to do with it. I mean, theists believe there's something after, something better than, this life, no? Or at least a second chance?"

"Yes—and you may have a good point there: as soon as you know that this is all you've got, all you'll ever get, you might be more apt to try and make a better go of it."

"Did anyone still believe in their Santa Claus after that?" Larah spoke up. She had followed most of the story.

"Yes, a few. But it's funny. Suddenly one of the 'Golden Rules' was 'God helps those who help themselves'," he chuckled.

They sat for a moment enjoying the warmth of the sunlight pouring into the room. Jeth noticed then that his grand-za's friend had fallen asleep. He realized his grand-za probably wanted to do the same, it had been a long afternoon.

"Well," he stood up, "perhaps it's time for us to go." Larah agreed and gave her great-grand-za a kiss good-bye. She climbed off the rocking chair and took Jeth's hand.

"We'll see you next week," Jeth said as he and Larah went to the door.

The old man nodded, then got up to wave out the window.

Fifteen minutes later they were on the highway, Larah drifting off and Jeth thinking about his grand-za's story. Usually he ignored the billboards with their inane messages stating in bold colours either the obvious or the useless. But now one of them caught his eye: 'If ye save yeself, ye shall be saved!' It seemed more than ever to be moronically blatant, a simple tautology.

Answer Period

It is morning. It is morning in Ottawa. It is morning in Ottawa, the capital city of Canada.

Frank Katsas half-ran up the many stairs of the parliament buildings. It was the half-run some people used to get from the wings to centre stage. Was it supposed to project an image of youthfulness, the fitness assumed to accompany it? Or was it intended to suggest someone in a hurry, with things to do and appointments to keep, someone, therefore, important? Frank Katsas, MP for the Liberal party, didn't wonder about that, one hand holding his new attaché case, the other holding closed the jacket of his three-piece suit. He liked these stairs. There were so many of them, going up.

When he got to the top again that day, he entered the first building, then walked down a hall to the large room where the parliamentary sessions were held. A look at his watch assured him that he was probably the first one to arrive, again. As soon as he opened the heavy doors of that inner chamber, he felt it: a sort of sacred hush. He sometimes thought, this is my reason for being here. He also thought his high school reunion should've been this year instead of last.

Judy Chan was also making her way up these stairs. These goddamned stairs, she was thinking. Such a naked manifestation of the hierarchical mode of thought, son of the linear mode of thought. On top of Mount Olympus, the gods resided. But since all they did was hurl thunderbolts at each other, they killed themselves off in no time. Nevertheless, legends of their heroic deeds live on in the hearts of mediocre men. Who are given thrones to sit on and messenger boys to do their bidding, no chicken and egg puzzle here.

She was short of breath when she reached the top. Nothing carbon-based can live at such oxygen-starved altitudes, she thought. If the sessions were held at street level, maybe more street level politics would be practised. People underestimate the influence of their environment, she remarked to herself as she entered the building and headed down the hall. Take these doors, for instance. Or the plush chairs. Or the thick carpet, or the chandeliers, or the table tops—mahogany? teak? The opulence was sick. And sickening. But, and, when need is out of sight, it goes out of mind. For what one of those doors cost, you could probably add another room at a shelter. Arborite and tile floor would've done. And folding chairs might encourage less dallying with the country's affairs. Whoever decided to hold arms talks at Hiroshima knew what they were doing.

Judy Chan had been nominated by her party, the NDP (the New Democratic Party), to run for office because she was a woman. She was also a member of an ethnic minority. So they got two, two, two mints in one, she had said, smiling. (She also knew how to speak French. When asked where she had learned, her answer—in high school—stopped them dead. They didn't know French was taught in high school in China, or Japan, or Korea. Viet Nam? If they were really slow, she'd say she didn't know either, but it was taught in high school in Canada.) (And if they were hopeless, she didn't bother correcting their next assumption, that she had been an exchange student.) At first she thought, the hell with them. If they won't even *recognize* my political skills, fat chance I'll ever be able to *use* them. So she thought she'd just say no. Then she thought, the hell with them. If *the people* want me to represent them, *they'll* vote me in, and *that'll* be the reason for my being here.

John Matthews was tired of climbing the stairs. And, but, he didn't have to anymore. As Minister of Justice, for the PCs (Progressive Conservatives), he had a parking spot in the lot at the side, which was level with the entrance. He was tired today. He was tired yesterday. No clown's feet, no ruffled skirt to wear on his collar, but a charade just the same. And he was tired of it. Oh, the job had its moments. Usually they were too few and far between to make it worthwhile; though any day could be pay day now. Trying made it worse because it didn't make it different. Division of power makes abuse more difficult, he knew that principle, but it also makes its use more difficult. He wondered, not for the first time, why he was here.

He walked down the hall, through the open doors and toward his place at the oblong table. The session was just about to begin. When he first became Minister, he had been advised to arrive later rather than earlier: it was a show of rank, authority, importance—let the peons wait for us. But it wasn't feelings of importance that had him arriving later and later every day. (And he didn't need the staff psychologist to tell him that.)

The speaker called the buzzing House to order. It became quiet—for just a moment. A member from Hamilton-Wentworth had a question for Thomas, the Minister of Finance. Then the North Simcoe rep asked a Toronto rep about dumpsites. Arlene, the Minister of the Environment, got a chance to say a few words on that one. Then a question about—about the recent hassle in NATO? NORAD? He was hardly paying attention. When had the questions begun to sound the same? When had the emotional vehemence become canned? These issues were important, of course; they were all important. That was the problem. Because then none of them were important. A crisis counsellor cannot be alarmed every time forever.

Context is all. Contrast. I need to be called on for trivial things. I need to decide what stocks to invest in, whether to buy a new car, when to cut the grass. But Madelaine takes care of all that, so I don't have to. So I can focus on more important things, these things.

The Trois-Rivières member took the floor then to ask a question. "Canada is a bilingual country. It always has been—whether or not the various parties in power have recognized that fact; and it always will be—in spite of the various parties who have been or may be in power. And yet French-speaking communities across the country must defer to the English and provide goods and services in their language, while the same is not true in reverse. Your government has promised an end to this injustice. Several times. And for several years. But nothing is ever done about this intolerable situation. Does the Honorable Minister think, along with the rest of Canada, that its French-speaking peoples are low priority citizens?"

No, that wasn't a question, Judy corrected, it was an attack. No wonder the response was so defensive. "Well, I don't think we ..." Questions call for answers. Attacks call for defences. Or counterattacks. And that's what was going on here.

She listened to the heckling, the boos and hisses whizzing by like plastic bullets. Not a very supportive environment, she thought, all this negative criticism. Do these people know nothing about interpersonal dynamics, human relationships? No, she chuckled, most of them are men. Furthermore, they were *expected* to heckle, to criticize, to engage in one-upmanship, to compete—when two or more are gathered together ... And most people do as they're expected. As children, they were rewarded for it. It becomes habit. Habits are hard to break. Then there's peer pressure—Asch, Milgram, Zimbardo. So the status quo is maintained. And then there are the laws of physics to contend with— the path of least resistance, a moving object stays in motion in the same direction at the same speed unless ... So homeostasis is achieved.

And yet change, adaptation is as necessary. For growth, for survival. (Did someone say something about growth? survival?)

She thought about entering herself into the speaking order to give a compliment and a thank you to the Minister of Finance for cutting the nuclear submarines out of the budget again. Then she realized she couldn't. She's the opposition. It would amount to treason to support the other side. As if each side was unanimous within itself over any issue. United fronts are never strong: they're always fake. We should be called 'the assistance' instead of 'the opposition'. It still has a ring of 'resistance' about it, but it suggests co-operative effort. It boggled her mind to consider for a moment all the intelligence and skill being wasted here on opposing, knocking down, destroying. And anyway, she figured, it would be a waste of valuable time. To make the compliment and thank you. Then again, she recalled that such comments actually did have an instrumental role in facilitating group action (Social Psychology 250?). They *weren't* a waste of time ...

Another attack, another defense. Frank reached for another handful of popcorn. He thought he'd go out front at halftime and buy a hotdog from that street vendor.

I'm here because I was expected to be here, John realized. An undergraduate degree in economics and political science, then law school. I'm used to money. I'm used to power. That's the kind of family I'm from. At our summer camp, we played 'Merger Maniac' and had mock trials for everything. Our guest speaker, an ex-camper, was an executive producer of films. Why didn't I become a ... teacher? Or open my own business? Because I never thought about it. I didn't consider those careers as options. In the same way, that Lisa Poetzsky back in grade six didn't consider being a doctor; she became a nurse.

'What are you going to do about the deficit?' 'Why don't you fine the polluters?' 'What are you doing to ensure pay equity?' You you

you. The attacks were always personal, Judy noticed, as if Harold Panzer himself was responsible for what did or didn't happen. Most likely it was a committee. Most likely it was really out of their hands too. But the buck has to stop somewhere. Diffusion of responsibility killed Kitty Genovese. And millions like her in every war. Us and Them. It was so dichotomous, you'd think there'd been no new thought since the antique philosophers who divided the world into being and non-being. But more dangerously, so adversarial. Where did that come from? From all the lawyers sitting in this room, trained in the adversarial system of law. I'll pretend you're my opponent. Though I'll call you 'my learned friend' and we'll go for drinks later. I'll pretend my guy's innocent and your guy's guilty. Though I know otherwise or I don't know. So why pretend?

"All right!" Frank cheered. Another point for us. He grinned up at his team-mate from North Bay. Boy, was this exciting.

The table thumping and cat calls were deafening. Judy was surprised the speaker didn't stand up, clap her hands for attention, and cry out 'Children! Children!' It was appalling. Her high school student council had done much better than this. They'd been more orderly, more mature—more productive. She wondered how many sessions it would take *this* parliament to make the spring prom happen.

Something really should be done about the broadcasts of these sessions, Frank was thinking. A colour commentator? Player profiles? A soundtrack? Yeah! That would do it! And the Hansard needs a whole new look.

John looked around him. He wondered what percentage of those present had law and/or economics degrees. Add MBAs and you no doubt have a majority. No wonder things are as they are. This country, *any* country, needs people with philosophy degrees, and sociology, and psychology degrees. Social workers, teachers, doctors, and nurses, and engineers, and homeworkers and assembly line workers. *Then* the government *might* be representative.

A blue collar leading the nation? He could hear his colleagues gasp. No, see that's the problem. We're not really supposed to be leaders. We're supposed to be followers. We're supposed to do what the people want. We're here for them. John, any of them will say, you've got it backwards. No, he'd insist. All we really need is three ministries: A Ministry of Information, to provide everyone and anyone with any and all information about any and all issues; a Ministry of Polling, to find out what public opinion is on any issue; and a Ministry of Implementation, to do what's wanted to be done. They'd shake their heads. He shook his head.

'I'd like to ask when the Honorable Minister is going to pull his head out of the sand and—' Even at best, the questions were rhetorical; Judy noticed that the people who asked them didn't even listen for the answers. So why bother? What kind of answer can it be anyway when it must be given right there and then, in the space of two minutes, by a person who probably isn't the one directly involved in the matter concerned? (This kind: 'We'd like to assure the people of this country that we intend to continue to do everything in our power to act in the interests—in the very *best* interests—of this country and all its peoples.') All you're going to get here is a party platitude. And everyone has every party's Platitude Book memorized by now. (Because they're all the same: memorize your own and you've memorized the others.)

A member from Huron County was acknowledged by the Speaker. She addressed her question to the Minister of Justice. "What are you going to do about CLIP? It obviously isn't working."

Good question, Frank thought. He shouted out a 'Hear! Hear!' before realizing he didn't know what party she belonged to. He squinted across the room to see her name plate. What this place needed was binoculars. Yeah, a pair sitting on each table, right beside the translation device.

Judy hoped—fat chance—that the answer to this question would be a good one. CLIP was the Canadian Legal Insurance Plan. Modelled a little after OHIP, Ontario's health insurance plan. Premiums were paid from a surcharge on federal taxes and people received certain (most) legal services 'free' of charge when and as they needed them. The idea behind the plan was that legal services were about as important as medical services, and since they were also as expensive, many people had to do without. The reality of this, it had been argued, was unconstitutional; it violated or contradicted the Charter of Human Rights, insofar as the rights guaranteed therein—for example, the right to seek shelter and employment free of discrimination on the basis of colour, creed, gender, etc.—were actually 'guaranteed' only if you could afford to take the transgressor to court. CLIP changed that. However, the plan went bankrupt almost immediately because so many of the claims registered were to take companies to court for personal health damages from toxic pollution. The companies could and did afford long drawn out court battles that drained CLIP'S funds. She waited for the Minister's answer.

"You're right," John said, "it isn't working." Every member of the PC party gasped. "And I don't know what to do about it. Do you have any suggestions?"

There was silence. The entire House was stunned. He had just done something against all expectations of self, family, friends, colleagues, the country, the entire world for god's sake. He had conceded. He had admitted failure. He had admitted ignorance. The three big 'nevers'. And then he had the nerve to ask for suggestions. From some lesser person who, on top of that, was a member of the Opposition. And, but hardly anyone noticed this, he had bypassed the

Speaker and had spoken directly to the person who had asked the question.

"Well ...," the Huron rep was floundering, embarrassed.

Beautiful, Judy thought. Now there's a man who's not afraid to—who's willing to—there's a real person!

John wondered for a moment what he had just done. Lost a bunch of votes? Lost his job? Was it irresponsible? He had a family to support.

Was he crazy? Frank was horrified. Then he was angry. I'd give my right arm to be in his shoes and he just throws it away like he doesn't care—wait a minute—I'll bet— The guy isn't crazy, he's brilliant! It was intentional! What a move! M.V.P. award for sure!

Someone, somewhere, had recovered enough to speak. "We could increase the premiums, the surcharge—"

"But the increase would have to be, I'm not sure, but maybe at least 1000% just to break even," John answered.

"That's too much—the taxpayers would revolt!" Someone else spoke up.

"*I'd* revolt!" another voice. It was comic relief—there was laughter all round. *All round*, Judy marvelled. They were all laughing! Not at each other, but together!

"What about a drastic cut to the list of eligible services?" another person suggested.

This is incredible, Judy marvelled. She looked at the Speaker. Please don't interrupt this magic moment. But the Speaker looked as awed as Judy, and frankly, relieved. She was enjoying this as much as anyone.

"Wouldn't that defeat the purpose of the plan?"

"Well, probably," John responded.

"I have an idea—"

Judy turned to find the voice—it was someone who had never spoken in the House before.

"Since the damage is being done mostly by the claims against companies, why don't we set a ceiling on how much those companies can spend. We *know* they're unnecessarily protracting the court process—"

"Or what about then, instead, on how *long* the case can go on?"

"Or what about both? I mean, is it fair for the company to afford some big shot lawyer while CLIP pays for someone just out of law school?"

"What if it *is* really an issue of backlog though—"

"We can appoint more judges—"

"I've been after that for years!" The Minister of Justice, John, grinned. He'd just grinned, he realized. When was the last time—

There, see? What's so bad about admitting failure, Judy was asking. She knew though. To admit failure was in essence to change one's mind. And that, though the prerogative of inferior creatures such as women, who could afford to be silly and fickle, was not the mark of a strong man. Strong as in oak or strong as in willow? Rock or water? It takes intelligence to recognize failure, and it takes strength to act on that recognition—to correct, improve, adapt, change ... To grow. To survive.

"Well, we're a lot of us here lawyers, how *long* should these cases be taking?"

"Two years," someone said.

"Three."

"Two and a half."

"Four at most."

"I say three."

"Two."

"Okay," John waited until all estimates were heard, "how about we say three years, four pending approval of application for extension? Agreed?" There were no 'nays'. Or hisses.

"All right, I think we have enough expertise in the room to decide on the cost ceiling right now as well. Let's hear an opening bid."

Judy was delighted. She was suddenly at an auction. And in just five minutes, the House had agreed on a figure.

"Great. I'll put these two changes into effect immediately, and we'll see what happens. In case this doesn't solve the problem though, or if it doesn't solve it completely, I'll continue to be open to other proposals—especially from any of you who want time to research and/or poll your constituents." John sat down. He was smiling.

So was Judy. Then she was clapping. Frank and a few others joined in. She stood up. Soon the whole House, the Speaker included, was giving John Matthews a standing ovation. He stood too then, bowed a thank you, then joined in the applause to deflect it from himself and onto everyone in the House.

Eventually the member next in speaking order was acknowledged.

"I'd like to ask the Honora—I'd like to ask everyone of us—what can we do about …"